THE DONKEY'S CRUSADE

JEAN MORRIS

THE
DONKEY'S
CRUSADE

THE BODLEY HEAD
LONDON SYDNEY
TORONTO

British Library Cataloguing
in Publication Data
Morris, Jean, 1924
The Donkey's Crusade
I. Title
823'.914[J]   PZ7
ISBN 0-370-30985-5

© Jean Morris 1983
Printed in Great Britain for
The Bodley Head Ltd
9 Bow Street London WC2E 7AL
by Redwood Burn Ltd, Trowbridge
set in Linoterm Plantin
First published 1983

To Herta Ryder
with love

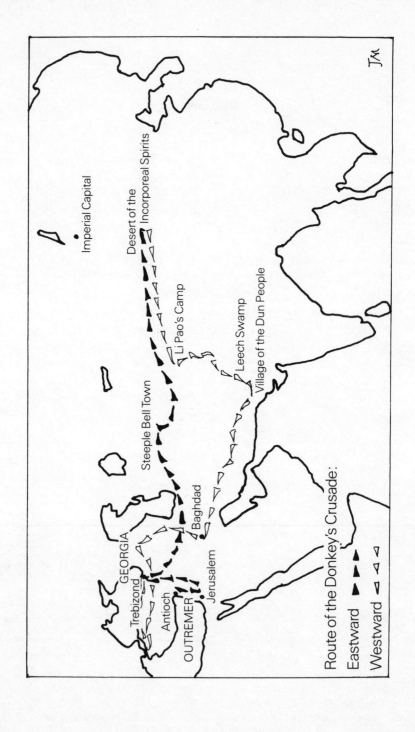

Imperial Capital

Desert of the
Incorporeal Spirits

Li Pao's Camp

Leech Swamp

Village of the Dun People

Steeple Bell Town

Baghdad

GEORGIA

Trebizond

Antioch

OUTREMER

Jerusalem

Route of the Donkey's Crusade:

Eastward

Westward

JM

I

Thomas's sandals lay beside the stone coping of the well. Every time he wound a bucket to the top, a few splashes of water damped them, but in the morning heat they were dry again before the next bucket came up.

Thomas's gown was pulled up through his belt and his sleeves rolled above the elbows. That was against the rules; but Thomas had sixteen rose-beds to water before noon, and each bed needed four buckets of water, and each bucket needed twenty-one turns of the handle to bring it up from the well, and that could not be done hampered by the heavy woollen gown the rules of the abbey laid down as proper for novices.

Under the shadow of his hood, Thomas was looking across the paved courtyard towards the rose-garden. He was feeling injured.

In the rose-garden, where the scarlet and white roses the Abbot loved flowered in geometric beds between stone-flagged paths, the Abbot was walking with two guests. Without lifting his head too far over the well-handle, Thomas examined the guests.

The one on the Abbot's right hand was elderly, with great grey moustaches, and plainly a Frankish knight. He was not (of course, in these holy precincts) armed, but his air was commanding and his knees terribly stiff. The long sweating hours in armour told on them all in the end. He did not seem interested in roses.

Nor did the other guest, who from his long grey robe, belted with a good wallet, and his shaggy head and great frosted beard appeared to be a holy pilgrim. He was a pace behind them, and looking at nothing; as far as could be seen, that is, behind the thorny eyebrows that projected over his eyes. The Abbot, as Thomas knew from other observations, was being his smooth diplomatic self, and if he was pointing out the beauty of his roses was doing so to give himself time to conduct a difficult conversation.

Well, that was his business. Thomas's was to water the roses, which in the summer heat of Antioch would flag and fall if he waited another hour; and how was he to do that with the Abbot and his guests in the way?

Eighteen turns of the handle, nineteen, twenty: twenty-one, and the bucket swung over the coping and set ready for the shoulder-yoke: neatly, to splash as little as possible. You do not splash water when a bucketful costs twenty-one turns of the well-handle.

The second bucket hooked on and thrown over the coping. The leather, soaked black and heavy, made a series of dull thuds which echoed weirdly up the well-shaft, and probably interrupted the thoughts of the grave trio across the courtyard; sighing, Thomas checked the descent–making his work all the slower–and allowed himself to slip off into his dream.

It was not very much of a dream. His fellow-novices, who were all heirs of landed Frankish fathers and owned such riches as silk surcoats, jewelled eating-knives, and even horses of their own, would have jeered at him for its modesty. This did not trouble Thomas. He knew the value of what he wanted.

He wanted a donkey.

It was three years ago when he had been sent to help Brother Hadrian the gardener. Brother Hadrian had once been a knight, and so had terribly stiff knees and could no longer get down to the weeds; he had to have help even with his prayers. When he had seen the extent of the work to be done, Thomas had put forward his plan: a garden donkey.

'At my home, brother—'

'You've a garden at your home, Thomas?'

'Well . . .' Thomas was more friendly with Brother Hadrian than with anyone else in the abbey, but even he was a Frank and ignorant of the real life of the country. Thomas's home was a narrow valley in the desert, where water was near enough to the surface for wells to be dug and cultivation maintained at the price of unending labour; no one there could afford the time to grow roses, but their melons and cucumbers and lettuces were the sweetest he had ever tasted. 'A vegetable garden, brother. We have to water all the time. And we have donkeys. Donkeys at the well–I could make the beam-engine myself, brother, with

8

a few bits of wood from the store–to draw the water, and donkeys with waterskin-harnesses to carry it. Two waterskins will carry ten times what I can on the shoulder-yoke, and the saving of time—'

But Brother Hadrian, who was nearly seventy and as a young man had fought against the magnificent Salah ed-Din Yusuf (whom the ignorant Franks called Saladin), had come to the abbey to make his soul in peace, and knew that there would be no peace if he had to squabble with the Father Prior about expenses. So he said bracingly, 'No one could work harder than you, Thomas,' and left it at that.

A donkey could, Thomas would have maintained; but he, too, knew that it was no good arguing with Father Prior about gardens. Father Prior was a grave man who worried about high politics, such as the perilous state of the Church in Antioch, beset with heretics within the Principality and infidel without. But so intensely did Thomas worry about a donkey that he could hear the *clip-clip* of its clever hooves on the flagstones as he toiled at the well; it seemed to him that if he turned quickly he would see it at his back, its heavy head bowed and its great ears twitching for the sound of his voice. He had taken the habit of talking familiarly to it as he worked; though luckily he had been for so long without anyone to talk to that he did not have to speak aloud.

'It had nothing to do with the case,' he agreed now with his donkey, 'that I *like* donkeys. I would have said the same if I had *disliked* them. The abbey would have needed one just as much if I had disliked them, wouldn't it?'

He heard the clip of the hooves as his donkey agreed with him. Bucket at the bottom: a pause to let it sink and fill: and his back into it to fetch it up. Two turns of the wheel, three, four. 'Hey up, Ears!' he said companionably to his donkey. 'Never ends, our work, does it? How many miles to Jerusalem, eh?' *Clip-clip-clip* went the hooves. 'Ah, it's not the Prior, it's the Abbot we should speak to, isn't it?'

This was a joke, as his donkey would understand. In his five years in the abbey, Thomas had addressed exactly twelve words to the Abbot ('Yes, my lord Abbot' three times, and probably inaudibly). But talking to his donkey always put him into a carefree mood; fetching up the second bucket, attaching first the bucket and then himself to the yoke, and straightening his back with care to keep the water steady as it hung, he padded through the courtyard and along the paved paths between the rose-beds, saying to his donkey, 'My lord Abbot (we should say, shouldn't we?), here is this garden that you enjoy—'

'And here is the novice Thomas,' said a voice in front of him. Thomas found that he was looking straight at the Abbot.

He had never before done such a thing. The first lesson a novice learnt on entering the abbey was to keep his eyes down and his hands folded in his sleeves. Even when the Abbot had not been looking at him—and why should the Abbot look at the novice Thomas?—Thomas had never dared more than a brief glance from the shadow of his hood.

Why should the Abbot look at him?

They were all three looking at him: the Abbot and the old knight on the path and the pilgrim behind them. And how, Thomas wondered in panic, did you fold your hands in your sleeves when your sleeves were rolled to your elbow and you were carrying a shoulder-yoke with two brimming buckets of water whose weight you could only just support?

'But this is a child!' said the old knight, apparently outraged.

Thomas decided to stay where he was. By bracing himself square on both feet he could hold the buckets still for a few minutes, and it was not possible that the Abbot should look at him for longer than that. 'Now if you were here,' he agreed silently with his donkey, 'we'd have no such trouble. Being a sensible donkey, you would have stepped aside—'

Should he have stepped aside?

'No,' the Abbot said conversationally, 'you're deceived by his size. Our young men in Outremer grow wiry, not brawny. Thomas, I believe you are already seventeen?'

Thomas realised that he had made an appalling mistake. He was standing in the way of the Abbot. How had he not seen that with his shoulder-yoke across the path they could not continue their walk? He must get off the path; he must get his sleeves down and his hands inside them; he must keep his eyes on the ground—

'Thomas?' repeated the Abbot.

Thomas side-stepped into the rose-bed, tore his foot on a

thorny stem, made a wild grasp at the swinging buckets, and felt the yoke tipping.

The Abbot and the old knight stepped hastily back to keep their feet dry. The buckets up-ended; the water slapped and splashed among the flagstones, beginning at once to vanish in curls of steam. Thomas looked at two whole buckets of water, forty-two turns of the well-handle, running away, and for the first time in five years his patience left him.

'My lord Abbot,' he said loudly, 'what this garden needs is a donkey.' And with mud all over his bare feet he looked defiantly at the Abbot.

He was sure that his donkey approved.

'You see,' the Abbot said incomprehensibly to his guests, 'he is not a child. He has at least a mind of his own. Thomas, my guests want to talk to you. We shall be in my parlour.'

And he took his guests back along the paths of the rose-garden to his lodging.

'Well!' said Thomas to his donkey. He was surprised that he was not trembling for his rashness, but the whole episode had been so improbable that he felt only cool and faintly triumphant (triumphant over the lord Abbot!). 'He's going to listen to me, Ears. Why else should he summon me to the parlour? When I come out, Ears, perhaps I'll have a purse in my hand to go and buy you.'

He disentangled himself from the rose-bushes, padded back to the well, and rubbing the mud from his hands and feet with the hem of his gown pulled it down to its proper length and tied on his sandals. As a boy he had never stepped under a roof without first politely kicking off his shoes, and still found it a dirty habit to go indoors shod. He knew at the back of his mind that something in his assumption about his donkey was not quite right; it seemed logical enough–or perhaps more logical than any other explanation he could think of–but he knew that the realisation of dreams was not as simple as this. However, just now it was a necessary assumption; it gave him courage.

'I don't suppose,' he said to his donkey outside the door of the parlour, 'that I shall be very brave. But at least he's going to listen, isn't he?'

He knew that his donkey had bowed his heavy head in agreement.

'Thomas,' said the Abbot, who was himself serving his guests with wine, 'this is the knight Reynauld de Cahagnes from Normandy.' Normandy, Thomas had been instructed by his fellow-novices, was the capital of Frankland; he held his wrists tightly inside his sleeves and bowed to the old knight. 'And his kinsman James from Normandy-beyond-sea.'

Thomas bowed again to the pilgrim, who said sharply, 'From England. Of Cralle in Sussex.'

'They are interested in how you came to the abbey.' To Thomas's intense confusion, he poured a fourth cup and beckoned him to take it. Stretching himself comfortably in his great carved armchair, he added, 'They have heard of it from your patron of Jebail.'

Thomas held the cup without daring to drink, saying, 'It was nothing, my lord–noble sirs–noble and reverend sirs. I mean, it was very kind of my lord the Bishop of Jebail to think he should reward me, but it was really his own fau—'

'He was new to Outremer,' the Abbot interposed smoothly.

'Yes,' Thomas said in relief; 'and he didn't know that you can't ride through a sandstorm, and certainly not in full armour. We had heard he was ahead of us, and when we saw the storm coming up I went out to look for him; that's all.'

'A most modest account,' the knight said complimentarily. Thomas shifted his feet in discomfort. He supposed that sandstorms were frightening to those new to them, but all he had done was to tip the silly Frank off his poor foundering horse and pull his cloak over the two of them with their backs to the wind.

'And he was kind enough to ask after us afterwards. My father had died that season, and the Bishop sent a message to my mother that he would provide for the education of one of us. I have four brothers, noble sir.'

'I must still have it wrong,' Sir Reynauld complained. 'I heard that the boy had been here five years. That would make him less than twelve when he rescued the Bishop.'

'I am a Traveller,' said Thomas. 'I was ten; I had been on the roads two years then, with my father.'

'Nomad peoples?'

'No. They have their village homes,' said the Abbot, 'but it is a guild of guides. Thomas's family I believe is well known.'

'But what experience can he have?' Sir Reynauld insisted.

Thomas took a good draught of wine and put down the cup; and his hands did not go back inside their sleeves; they thrust themselves, apparently of their own accord, into his belt and stayed there, leaving his arms akimbo in a way thoroughly un-novice-like. 'I am a Traveller born,' he said. 'My family have been freemen of the Guild for generations.'

'I meant no offence,' said Sir Reynauld, a little helplessly. 'This is not a guild I have heard of. And I have travelled all over the West, and from the West to Outremer three several times, and in Outremer by all roads from Antioch here in the North to Damietta in Egypt.'

The old pilgrim said suddenly, 'I have heard of the Guild. But only in wilder ways than I have travelled. And I have seen every shrine of the West.'

'Travellers,' Thomas agreed politely, 'are not needed where the roads are known. And perhaps the noble knight travelled to Outremer by sea?'

'*But,*' said Sir Reynauld, slapping his hand hard on the arm of his chair, 'how can you guide where you yourself have never travelled?'

There was a pause while Thomas considered his answer. How could he convince them that in his childhood he had learnt the landmarks for all the ways that Travellers had taken for as long as memories could be handed down? The landmarks were the legacy every Traveller left to his sons. And had they never thought that Guild members meeting in far countries exchanged knowledge?

He said at last, 'That is among the mysteries of my Guild. If you wish the services of a Traveller, noble sir, tell him your needs and he will make his own contract with you. How he carries it out is his business.'

'But Thomas, Thomas!' said Sir Reynauld: 'this is not a journey to undertake lightly. It will be secret, it will be perilous, it will take you farther than Christian has ever gone before, and—and, in short, we can't tell you where it will end.'

Thomas considered. 'A search, sir?'

'A search. And of the greatest moment. Thomas, I fear me you are too young.'

The old pilgrim said suddenly, 'The boy will do very well.'

'James,' said Sir Reynauld, turning to argue with him, 'you can disregard your own safety, but you will please remember what is at stake.'

The pilgrim merely looked at Thomas and waited.

Thomas looked him over. Whatever roads he had travelled, he had been on them for many years; he was all bone, skin, beard, and robe. But his feet were good, long, strong, and stringy, of a colour that could be produced only by years of weather and the dust of mile upon mile.

Quite clearly Thomas heard at his back a clip and stir of shifting hooves.

He bowed to the pilgrim and turned to the Abbot.

'If you will give me leave from the abbey, my lord, I will be pleased to make a contract with the reverend gentleman. I make only one condition. I would like a donkey to go with us.'

II

While the morning shadows were still cool in the streets of Antioch, Thomas was on his way to the Muslim quarter by the Fortified Bridge and the house of his sister Amina. His hands were in his sleeves again, but only because they were keeping a fat purse out of sight.

Thomas had survived his first year at the abbey because he had said he would; but after that because of Amina.

He had taken no notice of the Bishop's offer at first, beyond saying carelessly to his mother, 'Send Peter!' Peter was his next brother, and the clever one of the family; but there were three girls in between them, which made Peter too young for the abbey.

'And I'm too old,' he had pointed out to the family council his mother had summoned to discuss the Bishop's offer. There were always a couple of dozen Travellers in the home village: as well as mothers settled while they had young children, the sick and old took refuge there, and the young and able-bodied rested between contracts. It had happened that Great-Uncle Yusuf was there, the only surviving brother of Thomas's grandfather, respected for his age and experience. Where most of the family were in favour of civilly ignoring the offer, on the grounds that Travellers had never had much to do with the Franks and looked forward to having even less, Great-Uncle Yusuf had disagreed.

'These fools of Franks have been here a hundred and fifty years,' he began, and sent a sharp look round to quell signs of impatience; he did not approve of beginning explanations anywhere but at the beginning. 'They came to capture Jerusalem, no doubt, but they meant to capture a kingdom for themselves as well, and who blames them? But, as I could have told them at the time—' (he believed this so firmly that the younger members of the family were beginning to do so as well) —'having captured their kingdom they were never able to hold it, a little Christian field in the domains of Islam. They've been failing ever since their first successes, but they'll be here for a few years yet.'

He waited for someone to contradict him, and one of the cousins said obligingly, 'After their last expedition–that incompetent business at Damietta–there's nothing left of the Franks' kingdom but a few towns along the coast. The emirs can drive them into the sea any time now.'

'They could,' Great-Uncle Yusuf corrected him, 'if they wanted to. *But* they don't. For one thing, they know the value of the Frankish trade. So do we all who live here, though we all pretend we only have to do with our own religion. But the chief reason is that the emirs aren't worried about the Franks in the West. There's a much more dangerous enemy in the East, and that's the Khwarismians. The emirs will deal with the Franks when they've done with Jelal ad-Din.'

'And may that be soon,' said several voices, and even Great-Uncle Yusuf condescended to nod in agreement. Jelal ad-Din's domains in the East were for ever in an uproar of attempted expansion and no organisation at all, so that very little travelling had been possible there for years. Travellers were quite used to threading their way through little local wars, being allowed to pass because they brought trade and were strict in their neutrality; but, if there were prolonged wars, trade gradually lapsed, and if there was no trade there was no demand for the services of Travellers. Jelal ad-Din's wars had closed roads that had been open for centuries, and when roads were closed the memory of them was difficult to keep alive; and when peoples were not used to the Travellers they forgot them, and came to treat them as enemies.

'May it indeed,' Great-Uncle Yusuf said with an air of finality, 'but until then the Frankish kingdom will continue, and a Guild member with contacts in a Frankish abbey will be useful. Contacts mean contracts.'

This was one of the articles of faith of Travellers; so he had concluded the argument. Thomas went to the abbey. In the years that followed, he came to the conclusion that Great-Uncle Yusuf was right, but had under-estimated the difficulties. The mistake was pardonable, because no one of his great experience could have expected Frankish education to be what it was. Thomas was forbidden to speak Arabic, which was one of his cradle-tongues, because it was the language of the infidel; he was told he did not speak Greek—another of his cradle-tongues and the *lingua franca* of half the East—because what he spoke was not a peculiar tongue learnt by Brother Gilles from books in a barbarous place called Paris; he was rendered blank with amazement by their mistaken ideas about the country they lived in. The only places where he was both welcomed and happy were the garden and the choir, where Brother Hieronymus clapped his hands in pleasure to find a true ear and a clear voice; and even there took great pains to train him out of his skill in Arabic shakes and quarter-tones.

It had all seemed to Thomas the waste of an experienced Traveller; but then Amina and Hakim moved to Antioch. When they were first married, Hakim had had a good small business farther south on the Acre–Jerusalem run, convoying pilgrims to the Holy City. This, a job of delicacy on account of the religious complications, was well suited to Hakim, who was a large humorous man capable of settling any religious dispute either by his size or by his humour. 'This,' he would cheerfully say, holding the scruff of a Christian in one hand and that of a Muslim, or possibly a Jew, in the other, 'this is holy ground to all of us, so we'll all behave accordingly, shall we?' But not even

Hakim could stand out against the increasing bands of marauders who frequented the desolate hills around Jerusalem, where the honest bandits (of all religions) pursuing their professions were being replaced by dissatisfied Franks robbed of purpose by the failure of the Damietta crusade. Thomas suspected that it was Amina who had persuaded him to move to Antioch, for she had seemed uneasy about her brother ever since she had managed a visit when she had come back to the Valley of the Seven Trees for the birth of her first child. Before she left she had somehow arranged to have the baby (a boy) christened in Antioch, with Thomas as godfather. Hakim, though as good a Muslim as any Traveller could be, did not mind, for he was proud of having married into the family; and it was a gift to Thomas, for it gave him leave from the abbey to visit his godson.

There were difficult moments; sometimes it seemed that nothing could prevent Father Prior discovering that the novice's brother-in-law was a Muslim; sometimes, in spite of her welcome, it seemed to Thomas that Amina was watching him dubiously–when, for example, in spite of slipping off his shoes at her door and sitting on the floor to eat in the proper fashion, his hands would slip inside his sleeves and his eyes fasten on the ground. But her unease would clear whenever he became interested in the talk and spoke up; and, as the months and then the years went by (there seemed no reason to tell Father Prior that his godson had brothers and sisters without Christian baptism), the hours at Amina's house did more than keep him going; they kept him informed.

In those days Antioch was probably the best-informed (in the Travellers' sense) of all Outremer and the emirates around; for it was surrounded by Muslim lands, and unlike any of the other Frankish domains in being alternately controlled by and in bitter warfare with the Armenians from the hill-country to the North-East, who were Christians but heretic. By the time Thomas had spent an evening listening to Hakim and his friends exchanging Travellers' gossip, he knew as much about the state of the roads as if he had never entered the abbey.

But Amina in her quiet way never stopped worrying about him; and when he turned up this morning, and had not even time to kick off his sandals before he began, 'Father Prior says—' she plumped down the brass pot she was scouring and looked thunderous. Like Thomas, she was small and sandy, but unlike him she had heavy brows she could pull together to make a picture of anger.

'No, no, no!' said Thomas, too full of his errand to enjoy himself by leading up to a dramatic announcement. 'You'll *like* what he says. It's a message for Hakim. The lord Abbot told him to send it. Will Hakim please buy for us–and here's the purse, and you can see from the weight of it–*feel*!–that he's to get the very best–and everything necessary to go with it, tell him, in the way of harness, and oil for the harness, and a salt-block of course—'

Amina put her fist–her palm was all over scouring-sand–over his mouth to silence him. 'Brother–Thomas–what's happened to you?'

'I'm going to have a donkey,' Thomas said shyly.

Amina drew back to look at him. Slowly wiping the sand from her hands, she scanned his bright face, and then threw her arms round him and hugged him. 'You look like yourself. You're going on the roads again. Where, what contract?'

'East, far I think, but I don't know yet; a solitary Frank, but I judge capable. I can't stay, dear. You'll see Hakim finds my donkey quickly? And I forgot: in secret.'

'I'll see to it. You're leaving soon? A good journey, Thomas!'

Travellers never made elaborate farewells. When each contract could occupy at least a year, leave-taking could not be anything but casual, for which they were all thankful. Thomas put the purse into her hands, returned her embrace hurriedly, and set off back to the abbey. He had business there in the kitchens and out-buildings, where the porters and scullery-boys congregated. Though it never occurred to the Abbot, these infidel (as he would have called them) knew in detail exactly what Thomas had been doing since he stopped drawing water for the rose-beds before noon yesterday. If Thomas's contract was to preserve its secrecy, they must be supplied with a credible story.

From the windows of the abbey, now that the sun was westering, you could look down at one half-circle of the city walls to the East, and know that the other half stood along the mountain-tops behind you to the West. Looking down from the narrow-cut windows of the chapter-house, the Sieur de Cahagnes sighed. 'All so long ago, our old glorious battles! A hundred and fifty years ago the great Bohemond fought his way in to Antioch. Is that—down there—the tower where he gained the city?'

Thomas said dutifully, 'No, noble sir, it's too far to the North. But there, to the West of the Palace, is the Gate of St George, which was the first to fall.' In his view, Antioch had been gained, not by any great Frank but by the treachery of a little Turk; but he was too wise to expect any Frank to see it in this way. 'Is this your first visit to the city, sir?'

Sir Reynauld looked uncomfortable. 'The difficulties of reaching Antioch, Thomas—'

All the Franks were ashamed of the fact that Antioch, the first principality of Outremer, was now isolated from it by Muslim Lattakieh. Respectfully, Thomas did not point out that Hakim would have brought him from Acre at a very competitive price. He pointed out some more landmarks; but Sir Reynauld's face seemed always to be turned to where, past the little buildings of the lower town, the levels of the river Orontes reflected the cold evening sky.

He said at last, 'That way, Thomas—beyond the river—that's the way to the East?'

There was something so plain and honest in his face that Thomas stopped being respectful. 'To go East, sir, I'd go up-river a bit first. Is that the way you want us to go?'

'It seems so,' Sir Reynauld said after a pause. 'Yes, we must explain it to you, Thomas.' But he stood still at the small window set deep within the thick walls, and looked down and across the town. The shadow of Mount Silpius was advancing East across it as the sun sank into the West. The shadow ran across the Cathedral of St Peter; for a moment the topmost tower sparkled clear and then was gone; beyond the river the flatlands were dark and empty. A small light shone behind them as the Abbot came in holding a lamp high. Thomas went to take it, and Sir Reynauld left the window, shaking his shoulders and rubbing his hands in the darkness, as if it had suddenly grown chill. The Abbot nodded to Thomas, saying, 'My cousin feels our air from the desert,' and Thomas brought the brazier, lit a taper from the lamp, and set light to the dried mosses at the bottom of the brazier. As the fire caught and flickered, it made a circle of warmth in the bare stone room, like the light of a camp-fire in the desert night.

'I cannot deny,' said Sir Reynauld heavily, 'that my cousin of Cralle is not a man who speaks overmuch. Since he has accepted you as his guide, he sees no need of more words.'

Thomas said, 'No Traveller requires more, sir.'

'Perhaps. Nevertheless I prefer that you know as much as we do. It will not be an easy road, Thomas, and you will take it the better, I think, if you are not ignorant . . . I do not find it easy to tell.' He sat, in the flickering light, with his knotted hands upturned on his knees, and looked into them. 'I took the Cross on my eighteenth birthday, in the courtyard of my father's castle at home in sweet Poitou, eldest son though I was, the family fortune though it was mine to defend. Sixty years later, can I find it easy to admit that the forces of the West will never save Jerusalem? It follows then, does it not, that we must find help elsewhere. Strong help, and immediate help, and help, above all, from the East. Now East of Outremer, of course, are the sons of Saladin—the emirs you call them? and East of them there is another people—'

'The Khwarismians,' said Thomas, who had been in the lands of Jelal ad-Din himself, and thought good manners would allow him to save a little time by saying so.

'You know the name, good; and their lands, as I have heard from the best of authority, stretch farther towards the sunrise than Christians have ever gone. But the help we look for, Thomas, comes from lands unimaginable that are yet farther East than that. Let me tell you my kinsman James's story.'

He sat back in his chair, and Thomas heard his knees crack as he stretched them out.

'My kinsman of Cralle from boyhood took to the life of a pilgrim. Curious; but his father also had the urge to travel. My cousin, then, having visited the shrines of the West, two winters ago turned South to Rome. You will have heard of the difficulties of crossing our great mountain-ranges, the Alps, and it was an early winter; on the way he gave help to a dying pilgrim, who told him that he held a great secret: the secret—'

Sir Reynauld cleared his throat, straightened his old back, and took a breath for the better delivery of the great words:

'—the secret of Prester John.'

There was a silence. He looked hopefully at Thomas. 'You don't know the name?'

'No, sir. Prester—?'

'John. Presbyter: Priest. John, Priest and King.'

He looked hungrily at Thomas; who said, 'John is a common name, sir, in many languages. And kings are often priests.'

'Prester John is a Christian.'

'Oh. There are small Christian kingdoms East and North: Nicaea, Georgia, Kiev—'

As he had known would happen, the Abbot abolished them with two fingers, saying briefly, 'Heretical: of the Greek rite.' The Franks (of the Roman rite) hated heretical Christians rather more than they hated the infidel. Sir Reynauld more sensibly said, 'No, those kingdoms are small, and, like us, hard-pressed by the infidel. Prester John's Kingdom is very great, very powerful, and very far in the East. Tell us then, Thomas: too far for your Travellers' Guild to have heard of it?'

Thomas assembled in his mind what he knew of the farthest East, and then sifted it for what these Franks would be able to understand. 'Well: they say that the Apostle Thomas went East to convert the heathen—'

'He did, he did!' Sir Reynauld agreed eagerly. 'And that he reached the Land of the Three Kings who came to Bethlehem for the Nativity of Our Lord. No doubt it was their three kingdoms that were his first conversions.'

'But that was twelve hundred years ago, sirs. I never heard that he sent word back.'

'The infidel blocked the way,' Sir Reynauld explained.

Thomas blinked at him in despair. Was it really possible that he did not know that the Prophet of the infidel had not been born for more than fifteen generations after Saint Thomas?

The Abbot, who had been born a Frank but at least knew Outremer, said quietly, 'Before the rise of the infidel, Thomas, there were the pagans and the heathen Romans.'

'Yes, my lord; but neither of them stopped the caravans coming from farthest East. The Silk Road was always open.'

'Silk?' said the Abbot sharply. 'We have made our own silk for a thousand years.'

But the Silk Road was still there, as it had been in the days when the only silk came from the Serismendi of Cathay; and where there was a road there would be caravans to take it in search of trade; and where there were traders with goods on hand they would find any possible way around warring armies. Thomas murmured, 'I have no sure knowledge, sirs.' He meant, knowledge that they could understand.

'Back to my story, then,' said Sir Reynauld, satisfied. 'To my cousin's story, that is. This ancient pilgrim told him that in his younger days he had been a scribe in the offices of the Holy Father; and among the archive rolls he had found a letter from Prester John to the Pope.'

Perhaps catching a gleam behind Thomas's carefully neutral expression, he interrupted himself yet again. 'No, boy; we aren't sending you beyond the known world on nothing but the word of a chance-met man. Being impressed by his story, my cousin made his way to Rome, and there contrived to have a sight of this letter himself.' He tugged at his moustache in some embarrassment. 'I understand that it was a translation into the Greek. My cousin is a lettered man, and a man of the strictest honour; but I fear it is undeniable that these archives were not open for the inspection of scholars; I believe my cousin was–hum–not wholly candid in his dealings with the keepers of those rolls. Nevertheless, he saw the letter, and found its sense to be just as reported by the pilgrim. It is a letter from Prester John to the Pope, proposing an alliance against the infidel to the rescue of the Holy City.'

'We,' the Abbot supplemented with relish, drawing battle-diagrams in the air, 'attacking in full force from the West, Prester John with all his armies from the East. An irresistible military manoeuvre: the infidel will be crushed between us.' The Abbot in his early days had not found his holy orders irreconcilable with fighting for Jerusalem.

'Sirs–but–East of the infidel—' Thomas began.

Sir Reynauld waved a stately hand. 'We are aware that the infidel have an enemy to the East.' (He made an extraordinary attempt to pronounce the name of the Khwarismians, and

22

Thomas wondered if he should help him.) 'It alters nothing. They too will be crushed by the great power of Prester John. Listen. He signs himself *Dominus dominantium*, lord of lords, and describes to us his kingdom. It is vast and prosperous and peaceful; milk flows and honey abounds, all is peace and tranquillity and justice. And from this wonderful land Prester John himself is willing to lead his armies, whose numbers are as the sands of the sea (than which, of course, there is no greater number), to the rescue of the Holy City. Is this not a miraculous offer?'

Thomas found it certainly impressive; chiefly because it suggested a horizon wider than any Frank's. No Traveller would doubt a story from the far East simply because it spoke of vast numbers; they knew that distances and numbers in that great space were far beyond the Frankish knowledge. It was well known that Franks had an incurable habit of describing (for example) any army that could not be taken in at one glance as a confident ten thousand, by which sensible people understood something over five hundred men not in full retreat. He said cautiously, 'Noble sir, all kings describe themselves as great and their armies as vast—'

Sir Reynauld nodded briskly. 'Naturally so. Why should they appear at a disadvantage? But Prester John was looking for no advantage. All he wished, he said, was to kneel at the Holy Sepulchre between the Holy Father and the King of Jerusalem, as the Three Kings from the East knelt before the Manger.'

If such an act of worship ever came to pass, Thomas thought, he would advise any King of Jerusalem to be very careful indeed. Or possibly that advice should be directed instead to Prester John? But the Franks were desperate enough to try anything; and it was no business of his if they wanted to get themselves into worse trouble. 'Then, sir, why . . . ?'

'Was the offer not taken up when it was made? Exactly. Between us, my cousin and I made enquiries. The letter was—hum—not recent, though we could arrive at no very precise date; it must at any rate have been at least a year on the way, and, the scribes in Rome having changed several times—indeed, the Holy Father himself having died and been replaced more than once—, we could find no one having any recollection of the letter, let alone of the reasons for its neglect. But it is possible to understand this. It is only very recently that the position in Outremer has become so desp–difficult. And you will have little knowledge of Western politics, Thomas, but there are Kings and Emperors there with whom it would be–let us say inadvisable for the Holy Father to disagree. Illimitable as is his power as the Vicar of Christ, he has no troops of his own. These Kings and Emperors, at the time when the letter arrived, most likely would not have wished to invite the attention of a power greater than their own.'

'But even now—?' Thomas said discreetly.

'Even now,' the Abbot interrupted robustly, 'some of them would rather lose Jerusalem than give up one inch of their own sovereignty. You will understand, Thomas, why your journey must be kept secret.'

'I shall say, my lord, that I have permission to visit my mother, and that the Sieur de Cahagnes was kind enough to bring me messages from my family. But you'll permit me to ask, if you please: what message will the Sieur de Cr–Crolle? Criolle—?'

'Cralle.'

'—be carrying?'

'It is to be hoped,' Sir Reynauld said obscurely, 'that it will suffice. Not signed by the Holy Father: that was beyond my powers. But by the Abbot here–it must be explained to Prester John that an Abbot can be regarded as a high dignitary of the Church–and by one who for all his faults is of rank and trust in the councils of France—'

'I mean, noble sir, in what form? If we are to be secret—'

'Ah; well thought of. It shall be a letter in small space, and I will consult with my cousin on the best way he can carry it unobserved. Thomas,' said Sir Reynauld, 'I begin to think that the Abbot has chosen our guide wisely. Now, for your equipment. You have no need to stint yourself. Ask for all you can need, and of the best. I have no sons, my daughters are provided for; all I possess is at the service of this expedition. This—' He turned impressively to the Abbot—'may we not say–this Crusade?'

The Abbot said soberly, 'I think this may be called a Crusade, and more truly than many others.'

'I thank you,' said Sir Reynauld, very stately. 'All I have,' he said to Thomas, 'is at the disposal of this Crusade.'

Thomas said politely, 'You have already been too generous, sir. The purse you gave me will more than pay for the best of donkeys.'

Sir Reynauld waved away donkeys. 'If you fancy one for your own use, have it. I speak of more important matters. How many men? I'll pick them myself and guarantee their hardihood. Then, mounts for them, spares, baggage animals—'

'My donkey,' Thomas said in bewilderment; 'and stores for the first week; and some money, perhaps ten or twelve bezants. And I would like another man with me, because no long journey passes without accidents. My younger brother Peter—'

Sir Reynauld was equally bewildered. 'You would like your brother's company—most certainly, most certainly. But your escort! How large? How many men?'

Comprehension dawned upon Thomas, and with it, for the first time, a shade of impatience. Would they never understand? Politely steadying his voice, he said, 'Sirs, be pleased to consider! Our journey must be secret. You give me an escort of ten men; good, we are safe from attack by ten bandits.'

'Thirty bandits,' Sir Reynauld said stoutly.

'It doesn't matter. There is never a shortage of bandits. And to travel with ten men I should need stores and animals enough to tempt fifty bandits.' He omitted the more important argument that it would hardly be possible to get a Frankish escort two days out of Antioch before they lost themselves in sand-dunes, drove their camels lame, and fell foul of the local people because of their habit of helping themselves to everything they took a fancy to, and without payment.

'But the journey will be dangerous! Without an escort—'

'It will, sir. So we must go unnoticed. I will have my donkey, please, and my brother Peter when we get to our village, and a sum of money suitable to three poor pilgrims.'

'Ten bezants, from Antioch to Cathay?' said the Abbot.

'We could do it on none,' Thomas said crossly. 'Ten will save us a few days, perhaps, and make it more comfortable for my noble client. When it's spent we'll earn more. Three men with a donkey will never starve while they can work, and three men with a donkey and ten bezants won't be worth robbing. There is no safer way to travel.'

Sir Reynauld regarded him with dismay; but also, he was thankful to see, with a certain respect. He said to the Abbot, 'One old man and two boys against the East? Is this a risk we can take?'

The Abbot–who had had Thomas under his care for five years, little though he had seemed to notice him–regarded him steadily; and Thomas, who for five years had been used to think the Abbot the greatest of men, regarded him as steadily, and suddenly thought that after all he was very far from being a fool.

'Reynauld,' said the Abbot, 'could you send an army to Cathay?'

'No,' said the knight.

'Then we must send two boys and an old man.'

Thomas bowed formally to them. 'My contract, reverend and noble sirs? With my donkey, to guide the Sieur de Cralle in his search for Prester John? And thereafter?'

It was plain that neither of them cared to consider thereafter. The Abbot said after a pause, 'Might that not be left to Thomas's discretion?'

'No,' said Thomas: 'I need guidance. To Prester John and—?'

'And back again,' said the Abbot reluctantly.

'And back to Antioch. I am happy to accept my contract,' said Thomas, and to seal it offered to each of them in turn his hand, now out of his sleeve for ever.

III

Hakim sent word, discreetly employing a kitchen-boy who was nominally Christian, that the donkey, ready laden, would be waiting the next evening (which was in the dark of the moon) at the postern by the Gate of St Paul.

It was a comfort to deal with someone with good sense. Without being told, Hakim had assumed that Thomas would be leaving by way of the Iron Bridge and the Aleppo Road, but also that he would not wish to join any of the great caravans which travelled that road. Thomas, in the same happy way, assumed that, if Hakim met him at a gate, Hakim would be a friend of the keeper of that gate and able to pass him out after dark. Sir Reynauld, getting it wrong as usual, said, 'So that you can leave in secret?—good boy; the infidel must hear no word of this venture. And you had best not be seen with my cousin. Instruct him where to meet you at a day's distance.'

As if every Muslim in the trade had not been urging on Hakim the merits of his donkeys for Thomas! Half the population of Antioch had already entrusted him with their regards to his mother and family. Hakim had arranged the departure quietly simply because he knew that it would embarrass Thomas to have it known in the abbey that his brother-in-law was one of the infidel.

But, humouring them, Thomas gave his client the landmarks for the first day's journey. It would be useful to see how the Sieur of this place he still found difficulty in pronouncing could look after himself. His client repeated the landmarks, disappeared, and returned at once with his bedroll over his shoulder.

'Leaving?' said Sir Reynauld, taken aback.

'Why not?' said the pilgrim. His sandals were good, strong leather, well worn to his feet, and his gown had a capacious hood and sensible belt with a broad wallet. He showed them something that swung from a leather thong. 'I have the letter,' he said, and dipped his thorny head into the thong and shook it beneath his robe. 'I thank you for your hospitality,' he said to the Abbot, bowed to them both, nodded to Thomas, and strode away.

Thomas noted the stride with approval: slow and long and purposeful. Sir Reynauld looked a little crestfallen. 'Farewells,' he said: 'difficult at best. Though one would have hoped . . . But he was always a man of few words.'

The Abbot, who had grown unusually silent, said at last, 'You and I, Reynauld, have set this Crusade in motion. We must not hope to see its course.'

Thomas coughed politely. 'Sirs? My client spoke of a letter. If we were known to be carrying anything that could be seen as diplomatic, the danger—'

Sir Reynauld muttered something stubborn about escorts. Sighing, the Abbot said, 'Be easy, Thomas; the Sieur de Cralle is of your mind on that. A letter is necessary to persuade Prester John that you are the envoys of Christendom, but we spent much care on the wording. Since the great King calls himself priest, I can write to him as my brother, and the language of Holy Writ will convey our message in a form appearing harmless to the infidel.'

'And the letter,' Sir Reynauld added, 'is written very plain, without decoration, and stitched into a plain leather bag such as the unbaptized use as lucky amulets.'

Thomas looked hard at them; but they seemed so well convinced as to be downcast. With a gleam of pleasure he thought that his client was showing good sense.

His own preparations were not much more lengthy than those of the Sieur de Whatever (and he had the breadth of Asia to learn how to pronounce it). From the Prior he reclaimed the personal belongings he had had to give up when he entered the abbey: his Traveller's gown, belt, wallet, head-cloth, and bedroll. In the roll were his cooking-bundle, with flint and steel and salt and bowls, spare linen, a box that had belonged to his great-grandfather and was stocked with remedies for hurts and fevers, and a small bag with a tangle of leather scraps and cord and old buckles, from which he could make and mend harness and footwear. He slipped away for a few minutes to say goodbye (with real regret) to Brother Hadrian, who unloaded from his sleeve half a dozen packages he must have stolen from the kitchen: dates, almonds, honey sweetmeats, and, most welcome of all, the herbs which with hot water made the tisanes every Traveller liked to drink night and morning. 'Brother,' said Thomas, suddenly trusting the old man who seemed so sad to see him go, 'I commend to you Thomas my godson and his mother, my sister Amina. They would like a visit when you are in the city. They—my brother-in-law Hakim—'

'They are good people; they took care of you,' said Brother Hadrian, confounding him by knowing that Hakim was not Christian. 'I will watch out for the boy, for your sake.'

He came finally to say goodbye to the Abbot and Sir Reynauld, and took care to preface the awkward ceremony with the announcement that it was a superstition with Travellers never to make farewells. They looked out from the rose-garden over the city, and the Abbot said wistfully, 'It is a very great city. Thomas, I don't speak of princes and kings, but merely of Christian souls. Thousands of them live here in peace. In you lies the continuance of that peace.'

'Yes, my lord Abbot,' said Thomas. He too looked out over the city, where Christians and Muslims and heretics lived in what he knew was very far from peace. But that was no business of his.

To his confusion, they had gifts for him: a good new belt with a roomy wallet on it from the Abbot, and inside it a black-handled, very keen eating-knife from Sir Reynauld. It offended his sense of propriety to take gifts when he could not return them, so he gave them, between them, some packets of feverfew wrapped in scraps of silk that were said to have come from the far East many generations ago, strapped on the belt, repeated the terms of his contract, and just at dusk slipped out of the side-door of the abbey as Brother Hieronymus was padding up to lock it for the night.

'It's never Thomas?' Brother Hieronymus said, peering at the unfamiliar head-cloth. 'They said you were leaving. You've been with the Abbot and that knight. What have you—?'

'Visiting my mother,' Thomas said cheerily. 'Four years since I saw her. That Frankish knight, he knows my patron the Bishop of Jebail.'

'Oh,' said Brother Hieronymus, disappointed that the news was not more sensational. 'And your mother lives a good way away, doesn't she? You won't be back for months, then. We shall miss you in the choir, Thomas. No one sings as true as you. A good journey to you!'

And the door of the abbey shut behind him. Thomas did not wonder if it would ever open for him again. Travellers did not think such thoughts. But he did let his mind dwell for a time on the Abbot and Sir Reynauld sitting alone and silent in the lodgings. All they could do was to wait, and it would be a long wait. He could travel again; and he had a donkey to go with him.

At the thought, his trot along the alleys of Acre turned into a run.

By the postern-gate he made out in the growing dark Hakim's white robe and black beard, and beside him a shape—a straight back, a heavy head, an upstanding ear that twitched to the sound of his footfall—

Thomas was so faint with excitement that he padded up to Hakim, wished him good evening, assured him that he was well and ready to start, enquired after Amina and the children, all without daring to look directly at the burdened shape that stood so quietly at his side.

'Well, good; and here's your donkey,' said Hakim, a little puzzled. 'You like him? A young beast, but good; I guarantee him.'

'My donkey, of course,' Thomas said foolishly; 'of course I like him, of course I trusted you to find me the best of donkeys.' He was seized by panic. He had got his donkey, he was travelling again, he had got everything he had ever wished for, and he did not dare believe it. He fussed noisily round the harness, making unnecessary comments such as: 'Girth, crupper, just what I wanted, good quality but nothing too rich. Saddle-bags, oil, water-skins, salt block—of course you've remembered everything. And a fly-fringe, why, that's—'

'Amina's gift,' said Hakim, still puzzled. 'You'll find mine in your water-skins. Let's have your bedroll.'

They strapped it on the donkey, and Thomas apologetically handed over his own gifts, which were very little, since they had not been allowed personal possessions in the abbey: his old belt (which was still a good belt) for Hakim, some stolen roots from the abbey garden for Amina, and for his godson his old eating-knife. The knife pleased Hakim very much, because, although the blade was ground to a finger-nail's width, the handle was carved in white bone, and it had been given to Thomas from a family hoard and was at least three generations old. Thomas made a great worry about knotting on his bedroll, so that he did not have to walk round and face the long pale nose and deeply arched eyelids of his donkey. He was becoming more and more convinced that he was only the novice Thomas, good for nothing but singing true and watering the garden. What had he done, to let two Franks believe that he could carry vital messages farther East than his family had ever gone? He thought of making a joke to Hakim. He thought of saying, 'Hakim, this donkey is a Crusader. This donkey is going East to summon help to take the

Holy City from the infidel; isn't that a Crusade? Don't you understand that this donkey and I are going on Crusade to rid Outremer of *you?*'

He realised that it was not a joke.

He realised that he was now a Crusader, along with his donkey, and that his brother-in-law was his enemy.

He realised that he could not go on his Crusade. He took up his donkey's halter to lead him back into the city.

There followed a confused interval in which he was conscious only that Hakim was roaring with laughter and that somehow he could not get his arm out of the loop of the halter. When he had recovered his breath and his balance, he was fifty yards outside the walls of Antioch, with his donkey composedly trotting ahead and Hakim shouting messages from the darkness behind him.

'—and love to your mother, and we'll bring the children to see her one of these years. And make a good journey with young Peter! And they say Miriam and her man are ahead of you. And *salaam,* brother, *salaam aleikum!*'

'Peace,' Thomas tried to shout back, 'peace be with you!' He did not think he had breath enough to be heard, and he did not know whether he had said *Salaam aleikum* or *Pax vobiscum,* but he knew it did not matter. It meant the same thing, and Hakim knew he meant it, and Hakim was the best of brothers who had found him the best of donkeys, and he was a Traveller and on the road again with a good contract and his own donkey. With a loving hand he slapped the bony rump of his donkey.

'Could we settle to an easier pace?' he requested.

His donkey jogged down to a walk, and as Thomas came up to his proper place swung his heavy head and looked at him. Thomas saw very clearly that this was a donkey of remarkable perception. He had very nearly acted absurdly, and his donkey had stopped him. He foresaw that this would not be the only occasion.

They arrived at the well at sun-up, having taken it easy on a short stage. It was a good fertile well, well planted, and there were as many as forty tents pitched there, ranging from a few skins flung over three sticks to the palatial carpet-lined home of a princely up-country sheikh eating dried grapes on silk cushions while he waited for his morning tisane. The donkey stopped to take a long purposeful look at the grapes, and Thomas had to make such efforts to persuade him onwards that the sheikh became very much amused, though not in a manner offensive to anyone's dignity.

'I would offer a hundred bezants for that incomparable son of several she-devils, were it not that one so insane as to own him could not possibly wish to be rid of him.'

He spoke in tent-Arabic, the language of the noblest Arabs, and Thomas, with difficulty keeping his feet against the donkey's sudden decision to look elsewhere for breakfast, tried to purify his own kitchen-Arabic enough to reply with propriety, 'He would be at your honour's service at no charge, if he were not too lowly to grace your far-ranging travels, on which Allah cast the light of his all-seeing eyes.'

'Breakfast for two,' said the sheikh, and tossed him a bunch of the grapes—luckily a little short, so that Thomas could catch them behind his donkey's tail. When they had come to an agreement to stop and look around them, he called, '*Salaam aleikum,*' to a man teasing his cooking-fire nearby.

'*Salaam,* stranger. Oh, it's young Thomas-ben-Matthias. I didn't know you were back on the roads. Nice little donkey you have there. Selling?'

'No. Did your dad get over his fall?'

'So-so; hobbles but gets along. Miriam and her man are camped away Southwards.'

This was good luck, for his cousin Miriam had married, as his second wife, a prosperous Muslim Traveller with four sons grown and in the Guild, and was moreover a famous cook. Taking care to impress this last point on his donkey, Thomas led him through the camp, exchanging greetings at each little smudge of fire. Sometimes he spoke kitchen-Arabic, sometimes kitchen-Frankish, sometimes kitchen-Turkish, and, when it was not plain which to use, he politely spoke Greek, to indicate his conviction that his hearer was a man used to cultured conversation. Miriam's tents were pitched and all the rugs unpacked, which meant that they had come by long stages and intended to rest for several days. She had the stones hot and was baking the morning bread, which she dropped as she flew to embrace

32

Thomas. This convinced the donkey that they had stopped at the right place; he ate it all.

Miriam and Aziz waved aside Thomas's efforts to replace the flour from his own stores, for they were a lordly family and used to plenty. Miriam mixed more dough while Aziz and the stepsons, who had been called from their own tents to meet their cousin, admired the donkey and argued about his price. They sat barefoot and cross-legged around the fire, dipping the flaps of bread into the savoury steaming pot. Thomas told them, 'My client should be waiting for me here. He came in solitary.'

'There's a solitary camped to the East,' said Aziz. 'I marked him; he'll come to no harm.' (This was high praise.) 'A good contract?'

'Far East.'

They were pleased; a far journey added credit to the whole family. 'Near East,' said the eldest stepson, 'they're in for trouble if they don't stop quarrelling.' He told them several scandalous stories about the efforts of the emirs–the sons and brothers of the great Salah ed-Din Yusuf–to unite their efforts against the invading Khwarismians. When he had finished, the youngest stepson said defiantly, '*I* heard that the Khwarismians had given up fighting the emirs.'

The elder stepsons said, 'That's nonsense. You always get it wrong. Take no notice of him, cousin Thomas.'

Miriam said, 'Stop bullying your brother.'

'Yes, but it is nonsense, isn't it, father?'

'That the Khwarismians should give up?–improbable. They're a fighting people.'

'And if something bigger is threatening them on the East?' the youngest stepson muttered.

They finished their meal and said their goodbyes, and Aziz and the stepsons went off on their business. Thomas asked Miriam, 'How sensible is that youngest boy of yours?'

'He needs to prove that he's as good as his brothers. If he'd known any more he'd have told us. But no news is coming in from the East. I think something is moving there, though I don't know what. You should take care.'

'I shall hear of it before I meet it.'

'Yes, if you're going to your mother's,' she said, satisfied.

They gossiped for some time about who might be found at his mother's home. 'Peter we saw two seasons ago in Antioch. He'd been on the Armenian route with Simeon's second boy. If you don't find them at home, there are Simeon's others—'

'—my other brothers—'

'Oh, you'll find someone to keep you company. Yes, I'm glad you've decided to take another.' She did not ask him the reason for his journey; that was not etiquette. 'A good journey, Thomas, remember us to them all in the home village, and we shall hear of you in seasons to come.'

She loaded him with gifts from their stores, which the donkey eyed with sombre satisfaction, and accepted only the smallest proper return, and Thomas with his donkey set out through the camp to find their client.

The Sieur de Cralle had indeed camped solitary, laying out his blankets a hundred yards from the nearest tent. He was rolling them (expertly, Thomas was glad to notice), and gave them no more greeting than, 'I am ready.'

'Thank you, noble sir. This is my donkey. He can carry your bedroll.'

The donkey swung his heavy head to look thoughtfully at Thomas; and turned his back on him.

'He is anxious to start,' the Sieur de Cralle remarked.

'He is anxious to kick,' Thomas corrected him, a little flustered. His donkey behaving badly? 'But you are here to carry the baggage,' he remonstrated.

The donkey looked at him over his shoulder, and edged round to keep him in his sights.

Thomas began to dance a little with worry. 'But Brother Donkey! Please!'

The donkey instantly walked to his side and stood.

Thomas tied on the extra bedroll, swelling with pride. Had he not seen at once that his donkey was a donkey of remarkable perception? A donkey like that must be asked: not on any account ordered.

'If I may enquire, noble sir—'

'It will not be appropriate now,' the Sieur de Cralle said in his deliberate fashion, 'to address me so. I am no longer of Cralle. I

34

am Brother James, a pilgrim.'

Thomas nodded in approval. A pilgrim meant a holy man, never mind of what kind, and everyone knew that holy men might be useful if helped, or dangerous if offended, and in any case were never wealthy. And he was glad that he would not have to struggle with that Frankish name.

'May I enquire, then, Brother James, if you have any objection to a mid-day halt?'

'I will do as you advise. These parts are not known to me.'

'Well, they're Muslim parts, which means that travellers stop for the hours of prayer. On the road we don't ask a man's religion, or we'd never finish a journey, but we don't offend a man's religion either. If we are with Muslims, we stop when they stop; when we say our own prayers night and morning, or grace before meat, we say them quietly. But before everything we put the needs of the journey. We can talk more at mid-day. Brother James, Brother Donkey, shall we be on our way?'

At least a dozen small parties were getting themselves under way at the same time, with much shouting and terrible complainings from the camels. Watching around them during the first hour, Thomas was thankful to see that there was no big caravan near them. Such a caravan, which could take several days to water, could starve out a small party without even knowing it was there. It was not too hot for pleasant going, and the road, which here was as much as a hundred yards wide, in the shape of dozens of small tracks running through the scrubby land, was sound underfoot. Brother James strode ahead, and Thomas and the donkey padded behind. Every now and again Thomas patted his donkey's rump, or ran his hand down the short bristling mane, or dwelt admiringly on the tall strong ears that twitched to gather sound from all quarters. A small laugh of happiness kept rising in his throat as he thought of the beauty and intelligence of his donkey.

They found a place shaded by bushes for the mid-day halt, and Thomas unloaded the food bag and loosed the donkey's girth. He said proudly, 'A donkey like my donkey doesn't need to be hobbled to stop his straying,' and turned him loose. The donkey ignored the remark and grazed off.

They ate Miriam's good bread, Thomas keeping a piece of his

for the donkey, and drank the wine that had been Hakim's gift. Thomas began, 'With your permission, Brother James, I must ask you if you are carrying anything of value. We shall travel part of our way with the caravans, which will give us some protection, but when we are on our own the only protection we shall have is of not being worth robbing.'

Brother James gave the stately bend of the head which he preferred to words. 'I had some argument with my cousin and the Abbot. They thought it necessary for us to carry gifts to Prester John. It was not possible to convince them that this was dangerous; they are quite ignorant of travelling. All I could do was to refuse outright to carry more than a letter.'

'In your amulet, yes. I am very glad to know it.'

'Otherwise I have ten bezants and some packets of herbs: some of them rare.'

'Herbs? You're a healer?' Thomas was hardly able to believe in so much good luck.

'Not gifted: a little instructed. I have travelled always as a poor pilgrim, and have found simple medicines a help. If none is needed, and there is no charity offered, I work for my bread.'

'That's how we shall go.' But Thomas was dubious about the charity. 'From what I've heard of the West, a pilgrim can find shelter and food mostly in religious houses?'

'On the pilgrim routes; sometimes elsewhere too.'

'Here, never.'

'We shall pass no Christian communities?' Nothing appeared to ruffle Brother James; if he asked questions, it was from an austere and not very pressing interest.

'There will be some, though most likely heretical, and I think it will be wiser not to seek them out. Though of course—' Here Thomas was on delicate ground. 'You will perhaps want to make your religious duties.'

Brother James said, with remarkable calm, 'We should not put our venture at risk for that. Did the Abbot not speak to you about this?'

'Yes. He said Crusaders had dispensation, so long as we went to Mass whenever possible. I don't think the Abbot quite understood—'

'No,' said Brother James, without troubling with the detail of what the Abbot did not quite understand. 'Whenever possible: if it is never possible we shall still have done our best.' And he cleaned his bowl with sand, put it neatly away and began to tighten his sandals.

Thomas took his piece of bread to the donkey, turning this over in his mind. It was unexpected, from a man who had visited all the pilgrim shrines of Europe; but welcome. 'Would you make the guess,' he said confidentially to the donkey, 'that it was the roads rather than the shrines that he wanted to see?'

Brother James was already striding off. 'He's not companionable,' concluded Thomas, taking the halter. 'Well, solitaries are like that. Otherwise, I've had worse clients. And after we reach my home village we'll have my brother Peter for company. You'll like Peter. He should have had the education, not me, because he was always the clever one; but he was too young. You'll like my village, too. The Well of the Seven Trees it's always been called. There are more than seven now, because we keep it well planted, but they say there were always seven even in the worst of years.' How much better was this than the abbey gardens! His client fifty yards ahead and his donkey at his side. 'And crusading too! The last thing I ever thought I'd find myself doing. How many miles to Jerusalem, Ears? It will be a long journey.'

And at this Thomas tipped back his head and began to sing:

> '*How many miles to Jerusalem?*
> *Ten score and ten.*
> *Can we come there to rescue them?*
> *But not come back again.*'

He discovered a new side to his donkey. As he sang, his small hooves fell into beat with him.

Charmed, he said, 'Ears, you're musical!' and went into another verse. *Jerusalem* was meant for a sad song, but if it was sung marching, and some new verses added, it could go very lively.

> '*How many miles to Jerusalem?*
> *Shall we come there too late?*
> *I made time aplenty, said*

Duke Godfrey in the Gate.
I gave all my life-time, said
King Baldwin in the Tower.
We come, we come, Jerusalem—'

They were up with Brother James now, who turned an austere eye on them. Caught without a useful rhyme for *tower*, Thomas lost the beat and said repentantly, 'I'm sorry, Brother James. Don't you like music on the march?'

'I have no objection,' Brother James said distantly, 'if you sing true.'

'You don't sing yourself? Two voices are better than one.'

'I had a true ear once. My voice is dried by the roads.'

'It's the ear that matters,' Thomas said cheerfully, and began again: '*How many miles to Jerusalem?*'

In a hollow bass Brother James boomed out the reply: '*Ten score and ten!*'

'*Shall we come there to succour them?*'

'*But not come back again!*'

And the rocks around them on the road echoed and rolled the answer:

'*But not come back again!*'

IV

Outside the next town Thomas and Brother James had their first disagreement. Brother James would not go into the city; he travelled solitary, he said, and must camp outside. Thomas became cross. The stalls outside the gate had been set up for travellers arriving too late for admission, and were hideously expensive. He set his teeth against the shame of being so outrageously cheated, bought just enough for supper, and before dawn slid out of his blankets and reached for his wallet and sandals. 'I'll be back as soon as I can,' he promised the donkey. The donkey understood, for he whisked his tail instead of (as usual when a meal was late) raising Cain.

In two hours in the town Thomas had bought all that he needed, which included some good pieces of leather. A harness or sandal repair could pay for a meal or a night's lodging in most parts, and an ornamented belt or wallet, such as he could make by the camp-fire in the evenings, was a suitable gift for anyone encountered along the roads. Finally, laden with bags, he spent a copper coin on a drink at an inn he knew of as a resort of Travellers. This extravagance was justified when a squat black-bearded Muslim hailed him as, 'One of Matt's brood,' and sat down beside him. As a Muslim he should not have been drinking wine, but he said, winking over his cup, 'Good fruit-juice they have here.' The preceding season he had met a brother-in-law of the wife of one of Thomas's cousins, so was almost up-to-date with the news of his family.

'But I heard they'd taken you for education.'

'Contacts.'

'Ah. Contacts mean contracts. This is a good one, I hope?'

'Far East,' said Thomas, and modestly accepted congratulations. 'I'm looking for news. Do you go East yourself?'

'Somehow not, lately. There doesn't seem the demand. Well, you'll be the one to find that out.'

Pleased by his morning's work, Thomas finished his drink, picked up one of the stray brats of the place to help him carry his stores and arrived back in camp to find the donkey in not too bad a temper, considering that he had not yet had breakfast. The brat, instead of whining for payment, found the right bag and overfed him.

'That isn't a bad little donkey,' he said pertly. 'How much did you give for him?'

'Fifteen.'

'Too much. I could have got him for twelve.'

'Prices are different in Antioch.'

'Do you come from Antioch?' said the brat, his eyes gleaming. 'My father was a Frank from Antioch. What's it like there?'

Thomas told him a few received lies about the glories of the Principality, gave him breakfast and a couple of coins, and broke camp. They had been going half an hour when the brat suddenly reappeared, trotting behind the donkey with, of all things, a bedroll slung over his shoulders.

'Home!' Thomas told him.

The brat produced a fluent story, taking obvious pleasure in embroidering it. His father, he said, had been a crusading Frank–a duke was his first claim, but under Thomas's cold eye he reduced him to a knight. This knight, just before his heroic death in battle, had married a wealthy and noble lady of (a pause to work out in which direction they were not heading) Aleppo; who had then been robbed of her inheritance by a wicked uncle who disapproved of her marrying a Christian, and died of a broken heart, with her last breath commending her only child to the care of his grandfather in (another pause) Baghdad.

'I'm not taking you to Baghdad!' said Thomas, scandalised.

'I'm a good worker and I know donkeys. I'd come just for my keep. And I'm a Christian. My mother had me baptized a Christian in memory of my father. It's your Christian duty to take a poor orphan to his grandfather in Baghdad.'

'You haven't got a grandfather in Baghdad.'

'I might have, if I went and looked, mightn't I?' said the brat, grinning.

The only truth in this story, probably, was about the Frankish father, for under the dirt he had yellow hair, though his eyes were Eastern-dark. 'All you want is to see the world,' said Thomas, turning him backward. The brat clung to him, protesting, 'Why shouldn't I see the world, then? I can help you, can't I?'

The donkey stopped dead.

Since he did so in the middle of the path, Thomas fell over him. The brat gave him a hand up, and said with a triumphant crow, 'Look, the donkey knows I can help.'

Thomas stared at him, and then at the donkey; who stood immovable.

'You'd be a fool to contradict a donkey as clever as this donkey,' said the brat cunningly. 'Look–I'll prove it to you.'

He dumped his bedroll on top of the donkey's load.

The donkey neither kicked him nor bucked it off.

'He does think you should come,' said Thomas, wavering.

'Then that's settled,' said the brat sunnily. 'My name's Aubery and I'm a good Christian and I can play marching-tunes on my pipe. Want some now?' And he produced a wooden pipe and started a thin squealing tune.

Brother James stalked unheeding ahead; the donkey followed; Aubery skipped at the donkey's tail; and behind them all came Thomas, pondering the ways of providence and donkeys.

Could there be any truth in the story of the grandfather in Baghdad? The obvious answer dawned on him: his mother. She would have contacts who could find this grandfather (if he existed); if not, she would know a family who would welcome a spare pair of hands. Might she not welcome one herself? All Thomas's brothers were grown, and all his sisters married. Or there were old Uncle Abraham and his wife; or Yakoub, who must have retired now. Someone would give the brat a home, and until they had Peter's company it would be pleasant to have a fourth in their Crusade.

He called to the brat, 'Give us a song we can sing, can't you?'

'I didn't know any Frank could sing,' he called pertly back.

'I am no Frank,' Thomas said in outrage, and began:

> *Matthew, Mark, Luke and John,*
> *Bless the road we travel on.*
> *Grant us water, bread and meat,*
> *Give us shade in summer heat.'*

It was not a Christian song; everyone sang it, altering the first line to fit their own holy men. They must sing it in the West too, for from ahead Brother James joined in:

> *'Matthew, Luke, John and Mark,*
> *Bring us home before the dark.'*

'Two true voices!' cried Aubery, capering with pleasure, and put away his pipe and sang high and clear above them:

> *'When my footsteps near the camp,*
> *Let there shine a welcome lamp.*
> *Matthew, Mark, Luke and John—'*

Habits come easily when you travel ten hours a day, at an unvarying three miles an hour (which is the speed of the caravan, being the speed of the laden baggage-camel), across lands which change so slowly that only the Traveller notes the moment when the vast upward slope becomes a vaster downward slope. There was a thick white mist in the mornings, so for the first hour they sang, rather badly, to warm themselves. Then the sun would burn through the mist, and for a time the world would be fresh and clear and sparkling, and they would sing their best. They sang *Jerusalem*, and *Matthew, Mark*, and some hymns which they all knew but whose words were so violently Christian that Aubery made up new ones. These words were not altogether successful, for Brother James banned most of them at first hearing, though saying it was Aubery's upbringing that was to blame. He banned also some songs Aubery said he had learned from his noble relations: in particular one that began *In Antioch there lived a maid, Bless you, young woman!* Aubery said it was a very religious song, about a girl who was converted; the tune was good, but there were too many verses before her conversion. Brother James was turning out to be far from an overly religious man, being quite content to say grace at meals and a brief private prayer morning and evening, but he did attempt to take care of Aubery's spiritual health, and made sure that he too said his prayers. Occasionally Aubery declared himself persecuted, and sulked, but not, Thomas considered, beyond reason.

The last song of the day was always the Travellers' Song, which Thomas taught them, for the late hours of dust and thirst and hunger and the camp-site that was never level or sheltered or near enough to water and fuel. It was the easiest song in the world to sing, for its beat dragged the dragging feet after it, and the tune shifted only a weary tone up and down, and there were so many verses that no one had ever learned or sung them all.

> *So the roads go by;*
> *Just the stone under foot*
> *And the sun in the sky,*
> *And you, my brothers, and I.*
>
> *Just the fire in the night*
> *And the blanket warm,*
> *The last prayer said*
> *To shield us from harm.*
>
> *Just the dust under foot*
> *And the sun in the sky,*
> *And you, my brothers, and I;*
> *You, my brothers, and I.*

Long after they had stopped singing, they were still moving to the beat of the Travellers' Song.

Last of all the tasks at night, when he had banked the fire and tidied the camp and taken the donkey his piece of bread, Thomas would take from his bag his tally-stick and cut on it another notch for another day. The stick was a handspan long and circular in section, so that he could cut three rows of notches down it. It was surprising how soon he began to remind himself to look out for another stick.

V

They were some six days short of the home village when they met another Crusader.

For once it was not a day that would blur in memory to nothing but a notch on a tally-stick, for Thomas lost his way. Little by little the land had tilted and lifted until they were moving across a great bleak incline of shale. Somewhere ahead, he knew, was a canyon crossed by the Crooked Bridge, but though he found the landmarks for the bridge he could find no bridge.

Aubery at last pointed out some hanging logs on the farther bank.

'Destroyed,' said Thomas in vexation. 'Bandit country, then. We shall have to go downstream.'

By the time they had found a spot where it was possible to cross they were far out of their way and very wet. On this bank the shale broke down into a maze of wrinkled confused hills, and they had to turn back upstream. When the bandits appeared from one of the small valleys, Thomas was not much worried. They were a poor lot of bandits, a good half-mile away, and none was mounted.

'We'll go to meet them. Brother James, they'll respect you as a holy man; offer to heal their sick. They won't worry us once they've seen that we've nothing to be robbed of.'

Brother James said distantly, 'I have come to the conclusion that I am carrying in my amulet one very large diamond.'

For a wild moment Thomas thought he had misheard. Then he saw Aubery's appalled stare, and knew that they were in trouble.

Trust that it would not be discovered? Round the neck was the place for jewellery. Drop it under a stone? The trick was known to every bandit. 'This way,' he said briefly, and trotted into the lead with the donkey, who, abreast of the situation as usual, had turned the shortest way uphill. 'Over the brow of the slope there.'

'What good will that do?' said Aubery accusingly, swinging in behind him.

'There's a chance that may be the territory of the next village.'

'And will they be bandits too?'

The donkey broke into a canter, and Brother James put a hand on his quarter to help himself along. He was not a young man, Thomas thought anxiously; indeed he was no sprinter himself, Travellers being trained for endurance, not speed. Would Aubery be faster if they sent him ahead with the diamond?–no, that would be inviting pursuit.

One very large diamond–how in heaven's name had Brother James come to be carrying anything so perilous? When he knew the danger!

The bandits were gaining on them when on the top of the slope above them, like a sign from heaven, appeared the Crusader. He was riding armed but for the helmet that swung at his saddle-bow, and the sun glittered from him and his great white horse.

'A miracle!' gasped Thomas. The bandits behind them halted, and after consulting dispiritedly among themselves began to straggle away. 'Can it be a miracle?' he added doubtfully to Brother James, anxious not to expect too much of heaven; but Brother James calmly agreed, 'Most certainly a miracle,' and stalked onwards towards it.

'Oh pooh!' said Aubery rudely. 'It's a Frank who's lost his way. Listen, Thomas! Offer to guide him. It'll maybe take us out of our way, but the very look of him will be a protection.'

'How do you know he's lost his way?'

'Because he's *here*.'

Brother James reached the knight and bowed, not particularly profoundly. The knight at once dismounted, a little stiffly, and knelt to be blessed.

'A good Christian,' Thomas said approvingly, and trotted up to Brother James, who in his deep voice was finishing his thanks for the intervention. Thomas bowed too, and the knight looked them over with interest.

'These are your people—a guide and a page?'

Even before hearing his court-French Thomas had known that he was a Western-born Frank. He was a large young man, burnt beef-red by the sun, with the faintly outraged arrogance of his kind; Western-born Franks were always outraged in Outremer, by their dim perception that they were not as welcome as they should be. Thomas nodded to the description of himself, and was about to explain that Aubery was no page when the boy did a neat bow and said, 'At your service, seigneur,' in very fair court-French.

Thomas had expected to see attendants coming up behind the knight, but there were none. This was curious, for a knight alone could not even get on to his horse or out of his armour.

'If you will instruct your people to attend on me,' the knight said to Brother James (it would be beneath his dignity to negotiate with attendants), 'I shall be happy to offer my protection to a pilgrim.'

Aubery nudged Thomas, who enquired, 'Where does the noble knight wish to go?'

'To Jerusalem, naturally. But first to a castle hereabouts called Belle-Désirée. You know it?'

'I know of it. It is held by the Lord of Montbriault.'

'Who is dead. The Lady of Montbriault has sent word that she is besieged by infidel and needs help. Guide me there first.'

'Willingly, sir knight. It should take two days; perhaps three.'

'Make it two. And let the page lead that donkey behind. War-horses do not follow donkeys.'

Thomas looked round in alarm, for if the donkey took offence at this they would be in trouble. The donkey, however, was merely looking the war-horse over with a contemptuous eye. To tell the truth, at close sight it was not much of a war-horse. The heavy Frankish horses never did well in Outremer, but, even allowing for staring ribs and stringy flanks, it was less a charger than an elderly and anxious plough-horse. The knight gathered his reins and beckoned for someone to help him mount, which

Aubery did with a swagger, and they set off again.

Brother James was tactful enough not to lead, and the donkey consented to come behind. Thomas found himself walking at the knight's bridle-hand. Frankish knights seldom deigned to speak to natives of Outremer, but this one was very young and also very relieved to have companions, and once he was satisfied that everyone was paying him proper respect was quite ready to talk. They could address him, he said, as Sir Tibault, and rattled off a string of additional Frankish names Thomas could not disentangle. He was, he said, the younger son of an exceptionally noble and wealthy family of Poitou, and his father had vowed to take the Cross in gratitude for the successful outcome of a law-suit with a neighbour. However, further law-suits had then claimed his attention, and in the end Sir Tibault had taken the vow upon himself. Thomas nodded intelligently to all this. Of course he was the younger son; the elder son would stay at home to look after his inheritance. But, like all Franks, he was a hundred years out of date, for there were no fiefs or fortunes to be picked up in shrunken Outremer these days. Thomas tried a few questions to find out in whose service Sir Tibault had come, and Sir Tibault became at once haughty and evasive. There were those, he said, who took their crusading vows very lightly, preferring lives of sinful ease in sinful Eastern cities; he had scorned to stay with them. This made his position clear; he had come out in the service of some greater man, been dissatisfied with the prospects, and, happening to meet the messenger of the Lady of Montbriault with her appeal for help, had ridden off alone to get in first.

He had not even been headed in the right direction. Thomas found it difficult to credit the depth of ignorance revealing itself here.

'And now tell me about this castle. What domains?'

'Well,' Thomas began cautiously: 'no domains precisely, in the Frankish sense, sir knight—'

'Frankish sense? What Frankish sense? A castle has domains, or why should it exist?'

'In Outremer—'

'Do you tell me,' said Sir Tibault contemptuously, 'that Outremer can tell a Frank anything about castles?'

Thomas floundered. He knew quite well the reason for Belle-Désirée's existence: a large watering-hole at its gates, on the tribute of whose users Belle-Désirée lived. And lived very well, the first Lord of Montbriault having cannily dropped out of some crusading army to build the castle and establish himself and his heirs in comfort. 'I think the value is strategic. The castle controls water.'

'Ah, strategic,' said Sir Tibault knowingly. 'And the lady of the castle?'

'The boy may know, sir.'

'Yes, enquire of my page.'

Thomas dropped back to Aubery; who, bored with being left to trudge alone in the dust at the rear, replied fluently, 'She is as beautiful as the day, as rich as the Emperor of Byzantium, and loves above all else red-faced young idiots of Franks.'

'Aubery, seriously.'

Aubery produced the lady's pedigree, the fact that she had three young sons, and a rude story about one of her cousins.

Thomas retailed all but the rude story to Sir Tibault.

'Three sons,' said Sir Tibault, annoyed. 'Well: too young to defend the castle; they need a knight of experience at hand. And if they are young so must the lady be. Shall we make camp?'

We, in his view, meant Thomas, and Aubery was sent for to unarm him. 'You need not,' he said kindly to Thomas, 'put up the tent for me. It is warm enough tonight to sleep under the stars.'

'I don't carry a tent, sir. The load on the donkey—'

'Did I not say I don't need it? A couple of blankets will suffice. My page will bring you my cup and dish when I am unarmed, but let me have water now.'

Thomas obediently gave him a drink from their skins, and hoped that the night would not grow colder, for he had not burdened the donkey with extra blankets. He muttered to Aubery, 'How did even a Frank come to be without blankets?'

'Had them stolen?'

'No,' said Brother James, who was unhurriedly unloading the donkey; 'he thought this was like Poitou, where all places are within a day's ride.'

And a poor dull place that must be, Thomas considered.

'Aubery, he wants you to unarm him, and you don't know how. You'll have to ask him to—'

'I need no telling,' said Aubery, and skipped off. Keeping an anxious eye on him as he gathered kindling, Thomas was surprised to see the unarming going smoothly, and Sir Tibault talking to Aubery quite cheerfully. He was touched to find, when he had a fire going, that Brother James had without a word taken over setting out the camp. The donkey cast him a withering look to remind him that so far no one had done anything for the old war-horse; Sir Tibault was sitting comfortably in his shirt while Aubery arranged a bed for him. Sighing, Thomas untrapped the horse. It was a good beast and stood mournfully for him, and under the trappings he found the callouses left by the plough.

Brother James enquired as he passed over the cooking-bag, 'Will this new route take us far out of our way?'

'Not more than three or four days. So long as—'

'That will surely not matter.'

'So long as the knight stays at Belle-Désirée.'

Brother James was surprisingly sharp sometimes. 'You think there may be other claimants there? It seems possible. Would it concern us?'

'I undertook to guide him.'

'To Belle-Désirée only; and our Crusade has first claim, does it not?'

'Yes. But he's such a fool! How would he survive without us?'

'Ah,' said Brother James, and set it out logically. 'His claim on us is Christian charity? Not, I think, gratitude; his appearance saved us from the bandits, but ours saved him from perishing in the desert. But he would not be a welcome addition to our party. Let us hope it will not be necessary.'

Aubery came back for Sir Tibault's supper, saying crossly, 'He's got a water-skin with wine in it, but does it occur to him to share it?–no.' After a time he staggered back under the weight of Sir Tibault's entire armour, and announced furiously, 'It is now his page's duty to burnish this. Thomas, how long do we have to tolerate him?'

'We've got wine too,' said Thomas, trying to sound cheerful. It was the last of Hakim's parting-gift; every wise Traveller kept a small treat in the bottom of his bag.

48

'And now,' he said when they had scoured their bowls and drawn close to the fire as the night chill grew sharper: 'first and most important, Brother James. This diamond.'

'Speak quietly.' Brother James lay back, shifting, as was his habit, until he could see the Eastern stars. 'I am sorry, Thomas. I put too much faith in the understanding of the Abbot and my cousin of Cahagnes. I could carry only a message, I told them, and did not see that they gave in too easily. It was not until today that it became clear to me that the message they gave me must contain also a gift.'

'Why?' demanded Aubery, scuffling about to find fine sand for scouring.

'Because a gift is the ambassador's passport,' Brother James returned simply. 'If I come bearing a great diamond, then I am the trusted emissary of a great man. If I do not, I could be anything.'

'But—' said Thomas, stammering as he realised how this truth had escaped him— 'Brother James, why should it be a diamond?'

'You heard my cousin of Cahagnes say that he had given the whole of his wealth to the search for Prester John? The pride of the Cahagnes family is one great diamond given by the Emperor of Byzantium to that Sieur de Cahagnes who fought at the capture of Jerusalem.'

'If we are to have our throats cut,' Aubery said cheerfully, 'it will be a comfort that it was for the sake of an Emperor's gift. Can I see it? I've never seen a diamond.'

'No,' said Brother James tranquilly. 'Not with that landless and lordless young knight over there. I would not care to lead him into sin.'

Aubery snorted in contempt. 'He's no danger. He can't get in or out of his armour without us, and he has no idea where he is.'

'He might find allies. In Belle-Désirée.'

'And he's stupid enough not to know how helpless he is.' Thomas sighed. 'Brother James is right; no word about it, please. And we must hope that they'll need him in Belle-Désirée.'

'And meantime we must sleep,' said Brother James, and rolled himself into his blanket and did so.

Considering the incidents of the day as he helped Aubery with his burnishing, Thomas felt wonderfully cheered. They had endured their first danger, and now he led a party, not four individuals. And between them they had some valuable skills. How, for example, did Aubery know how to unarm a knight and clean his armour?

'My dad,' said Aubery between grumbles, 'was a mounted sergeant in some Flemish troop. Or it may have been one of my mum's boy-friends; I forget.'

'What became of your noble Frankish father?'

'I changed my mind. Do you think I'd be the son of the likes of Sir Tibault? And another boy-friend was an armourer.' He was falling asleep as he worked. Thomas twitched the blanket over him, finished the armour, saw to the fire, took the donkey and the old war-horse their pieces of bread, and finally rolled himself as best he could in his single blanket.

'We've done well today,' he said to the donkey. 'Don't you worry, the four of us are going to be all right.'

The donkey, sombrely chewing, looked at him as if to remind him of something he had missed. He was all but asleep before he realised what it was.

Aubery was not one of the four of them. Aubery was not going on the Crusade. In fact, Aubery should not have known that they were going on a Crusade.

VI

As anyone might have foreseen, it was the donkey who rescued Belle-Désirée.

Sir Tibault did not see it quite like that, but by that time Thomas had lost any hope that Sir Tibault would ever see anything as it was. Drawing rein for his first sight of the castle, from the rocky ridge above it, he did not even see that the gates were wide open and the white-robed figures swarming around them plainly doing some brisk trading.

'The besieging infidel army!' he cried in satisfaction, and couching his lance sang out a battle-cry and struck his heels into his mount's sides. His tactic was simple: to thunder down on the infidel; but they had covered fifteen miles already that day, and the slope was steep and littered with stones, and all that happened was that the old war-horse backed and shied and shook its head violently. The donkey was equal to the situation. Twitching his halter from Thomas's hands, he positioned himself carefully and launched both hind feet into the horse's rump. The horse went thundering downhill, and Sir Tibault, after an interval in which he seemed grateful for the high pommel of his saddle, got his lance back into position and delivered a beautiful charge. It was not really spoilt by the fact that there was no one left to meet it. The white-robed figures had prudently melted away several minutes before.

'It had to be done, Ears,' said Thomas, patting him, 'and you were as gentle as possible to him. I think we shall be able to leave our knight here. After that charge, the Lady of Montbriault is bound to welcome him as a rescuer.'

'She didn't look as if she needed a rescuer,' Aubery said pessimistically as they picked their way down.

'Well, of course she'd carry on business as best she could. But sooner or later the tribesmen will demand their water at a cheaper rate, and having an armed knight in residence will protect her from that. Brother James, you're the only one likely to talk to her. Mind you point that out.'

'I have had little converse with women,' Brother James remarked austerely. 'They are said to be light-minded and full of vanities. On the other hand, she appears to have her domain in good order.'

The gates of Belle-Désirée had been hurriedly closed, and now they swung slowly open, and out of them came a very creditable procession. At the head of it paced the lady of the castle on her white palfrey. Her dress was white, her veil silver, and her hair golden and curling, and she was certainly young, though perhaps not as young as Sir Tibault. Behind her was her maid on foot, equally golden-haired and much younger, and behind her her three sons, all fine boys and certainly not old enough to defend a castle. They were in the care of three more maids, who were black-haired and veiled and having trouble in keeping them quiet. Trotting to take his place behind the knight, Thomas heard the boys demanding in fluent tent-Arabic, 'Why has that horrible knight driven the sweetmeat man away?'

Sir Tibault, blithely unaware of all this, gallantly dismounted before the lady, who hailed him as her rescuer, allowed him to dismount her, curtsied very low, and invited him to enter her castle and regard it and everything in it as his own.

'With the best will in the world,' said Sir Tibault, and no doubt glowed with pleasure, except that no glow could change the beef-red sunburn of his face. It was only at the last moment, and because Thomas and the donkey were in his way, that he remembered to add, 'I am escorting a holy pilgrim, and I have a guide and a page. May I recommend them all to your care?'

Brother James bowed to the lady and went in with the knight. Aubery had the presence of mind to cling to the reins of the old war-horse, and as the knight's charger had to have the same treatment as the knight they got a splendid stable in the cellars, with as much as they chose to take of fodder for the beasts and bedding for them all. A stable-boy offered to see if he could find them a bite of supper; but presently staggered back with such an array of dishes that Thomas prudently enquired, 'Mind if we put some of this in our wallets?'

'No need,' said the boy. 'We're well found here, and I've been told to tell you: you're welcome to take as much as you can carry when you leave.'

Thomas and Aubery exchanged glances. 'Who told you to tell us? The lady?'

'Not exactly. The steward.'

'We can take stores for how many?'

'One knight, three attendants, two mounts,' said the boy, grinning. 'Come now; you're not Franks, and you can see the situation here. What do we want with an ignorant young fool of a knight here?'

'You need protection,' Thomas said earnestly. 'He's ignorant, I grant you, but you and your lady can teach him. Your lady's no fool, the state of these cellars shows that, but she can't fight. Think of your future! You need a fighting man in command.'

'We have one ready. Those tribesmen out there have a chieftain. Do you think he'd miss a chance like that—a nice young wife and the Belle-Désirée tribute?'

'A Muslim?'

'Why not?'

'She sent for Christian help,' said Thomas as a last hope.

The boy burst out laughing. 'Of course she did. You said she was no fool. The chieftain has a couple of wives already, and she wants assurance that she'll be chief wife and her sons inherit the castle. She knew she'd get a better bargain if she could threaten Christian interference.'

Aubery, who had been looking thoughtful, asked, 'What's he like, this chieftain?'

'Put your finger on the problem,' said the boy cheerfully. 'He has everything but youth and good looks, and we're afraid that our lady might fancy your knight instead. We wouldn't like that; we want to keep on good terms with our families out there. Take your knight away quickly, please, and we'll see you don't regret it. Sleep well, and no need to hurry in the morning; we keep easy hours here.'

As he went out, to their surprise Brother James came in.

'We thought you would be dining with the nobility.'

'The lady and her maid,' said Brother James with distaste, 'are diverting the knight with music and dance. And we have matters to discuss. Are we private?'

Aubery went on a tour of the cellars to be sure, while Thomas helped Brother James to supper and told him of their conversation with the stable-boy. 'Such was my conclusion,' said Brother James, wiping his lips austerely. 'I will add from my own observation that the lady is by no means indifferent to the knight. I believe I have had a sight of the Muslim chieftain, who appeared to be speaking with the steward at the gate. He is squat and squint-eyed, alas. I judge the lady considerably our knight's senior, and very well used to having her own way.'

Aubery, who had come back to glut himself on sweetmeats, said malevolently, 'Not for *one more day* will I be his page. Thomas, if they won't have him here, what do you propose to do with him? Join his Crusade, or invite him to join ours?'

'Neither is possible,' Brother James said concisely.

'We'll have to leave him,' Aubery decided pleasurably, 'in the middle of the desert.'

Sad, Thomas said nothing. If they left Sir Tibault alone, he would be dead within a day, still invincibly ignorant of his ignorance. For that reason he could not leave him.

'There is also,' Brother James reminded them, 'the old war-horse. He has plainly worked out almost his allotted span in the fields of Poitou, yet he steps out valiantly. But now we have another problem to consider.'

He bowed his thorny head and pulled over it the leather thong that held his amulet. They watched in silence as he took his knife-point to unpick it.

Inside the soft leather was another packet in oiled silk, and then cream-coloured silk very thickly wrapped. 'That,' he said imperturbably, 'is why I did not feel the diamond. Ah!'—for he had come to the final layer, a bag of scarlet silk sewn in gold on to a small parchment with a seal. Brother James calmly cut the gold stitches, and held up between his lean thumb and forefinger something that flashed amazingly in the little yellow flame of their lamp.

Aubery blew out his breath in admiration. Brother James said, 'A fitting present from Christendom to Prester John.'

'And all the armies of Christendom,' said Thomas, tight-lipped with anger, 'could not get that diamond where we have to go. It could be the death of us all. And I accepted the contract!'

'*I* accepted the diamond,' said Brother James, 'though unknowing.' With his knife he started to dig a hole in the cellar floor.

Thomas stopped him. 'I have my contract,' he said.

It was not easy to make them understand him, but in the end they had to accept his word that this was the code of the Travellers. They took off the donkey's brow-band; in the cellars they found trappings of the castle horses and camels, and with knife-points lifted a stud here and a fancy buckle there, and, thriftily using the gold thread from the amulet, devised a brow-band that would take the eye of any thief. Meantime Aubery, who had the smallest fingers, cut the buckle from the donkey's girth, hacked and frayed it, and lashed it back with a mend so botched and clumsy that the greatest diamond in Outremer could lie hidden inside it.

Brother James knotted a ragged thread around the parchment, put it back in his amulet and the amulet round his neck, and buried the fragments of silk in the floor. 'And now the donkey carries the hope of Christendom,' he said.

Thomas was sure that the donkey was equal to that. But he could not see how even the donkey could save the Crusade from the company of Sir Tibault.

VII

The steward said pressingly to Thomas, after breakfast the next morning, 'Good Traveller, I would welcome your opinion on a war-horse we have in the stables. Is it suitable for my lady to offer as a parting-gift to your knight?'

Confused in his loyalties to the Crusade and to the old war-horse, Thomas objected, 'The knight has his own mount.'

'The lady can't let him go without something to show her gratitude, can she?' said the steward. 'I ask your advice, good Traveller, because we realise that you came out of your way to help us, and we wouldn't want to delay you further. The next water-hole is eight hours away, but I've told them to make you a gift of extra water-skins, and though we don't want to hurry you we feel you should start soon on such a long stage.'

The three sons of the lady were tumbling about in the court-yard with a taggle of dark-eyed children, shrieking in kitchen-Arabic, and all three of them were wearing new jewelled belts with charming toy daggers in them. Helpless, Thomas watched while a handsome bay was brought out and led up and down, and said he found it eminently suitable for his knight. The old war-horse was there too, in only a head-collar, and looking bewildered.

Aubery murmured to Thomas, 'Look, our knight and the lady. She hasn't made up her mind.'

The lady's hair today was even more golden and curling, and her dress richer, but she did not look happy. Her pretty golden-haired maid was not with her. Her sons, very sticky around the mouth, leapt upon her shouting that the sweetmeat man had

55

come back bearing many gifts, and the grooms hustled the bay in front of Sir Tibault.

'Pray try him at your leisure,' the lady urged him. Sir Tibault, with great pleasure and no sense at all of the pressures around him, mounted the bay, trotted him round the courtyard, and spurred him out of the gate. Aubery groaned softly. The moment he was out of sight the grooms brought from some hidden corner a great *mehari*, a trotting camel, trapped in scarlet and gold.

'A gift, my lady,' they announced.

The three boys swarmed over it with screams of pleasure in Arabic. 'From Achmet, oh madam mother, from Achmet, isn't he kind? What wonderful gifts Achmet sends you! Why didn't he come to dinner as usual last night? And look, he sent us these belts this morning, all jewelled. Can we go quickly to see Achmet?'

The lady's pretty maid advanced purposefully, carrying a roll of blue silk gauze all sewn with gold stars. 'A gift from Achmet,' she said in Arabic.

The lady looked with imploring eyes at her people; and her people looked stonily back at her. The lady lost. There were, after all, a lot of them, and only one of her, and her sons were against her.

She said to them, 'Where is the messenger who brought the silk and the *mehari*? I wish to send him back with a token of my regard.'

Everyone sighed: her people with relief, Thomas and Aubery and Brother James (who had appeared behind her) in despair. Sir Tibault reappeared in the gateway, cantered up to the lady, and, as usual wholly ignorant of what anyone else was feeling, called gaily, 'A magnificent mount!'

'You like him?' said the lady. 'Then pray take him, my dear knight, to remind you of Belle-Désirée and to aid you in your quest for the Holy City. And with him my every wish for your success and safety.'

And she stepped up to the knight to give him her hand to kiss, and over her shoulder said sharply to the grooms, 'Load, and quickly!'

They had started before she spoke. Thomas had expected Sir Tibault at least to show some regret at being thus summarily dismissed; but he was playing with his new horse, and had not even noticed that he had lost a wife and a castle and a handsome income.

'Let my attendants be summoned,' was all he said.

Aubery seized Thomas's arm and said furiously under his breath, 'Refuse, refuse!'

Thomas wearily shook his head. 'I can't,' he said, and went to see that the donkey was properly laden.

'We will make now,' Sir Tibault announced, 'for Jerusalem. Thanks to the generosity of this lady, I now own two horses as well as a donkey. My old horse can carry my armour.'

The old war-horse sighed and drooped his mournful head.

'Guide, are you ready?'

Thomas said, 'My donkey is ready.'

The donkey gave him a sombre glance, turned deliberately to face away from Jerusalem, and bolted.

VIII

It was nice to camp, that night, in their usual way, Aubery collecting the firewood, Thomas unloading the donkey, Brother James kindling the fire: no knight to take the best of their food, most of the blankets, and all of their patience. Aubery, on whom the brunt of his presence had fallen, went wild, capering through the sand, kicking it up in swathes and shouting a new verse to the Travellers' Song—a poor verse, but *extempore*.

> *'Just the sand underfoot*
> *To dance upon,*
> *No armour to burnish,*
> *No supper to furnish,*
> *No fool to ply*
> *With all we own.*
> *Just you, my brothers,*
> *Just you, my brothers,*
> *Just you, my brothers, and I!'*

To everyone's astonishment, the donkey uttered some odd hiccuping sounds, threw a buck, and set off after Aubery, galloping in circles showing his upper teeth.

'Well!' said Thomas, taken aback. 'If the donkey thinks we did right, I suppose we did.'

'Even codes of honour,' Brother James said austerely, 'can be carried too far.'

Thomas would not gainsay the donkey, but he was overcome by more scruples as he unpacked the saddle-bags. 'Look at the gifts they packed for us, when they thought we were going to take our knight away!'

'They could spare them.'

'And it wasn't our fault that we took them,' said Aubery, coming up with his arm round the donkey's neck. 'It was a good five miles before we caught up with Brother Ears.'

Thomas was beginning to suspect that the donkey did not like being called Ears. Or perhaps he felt he had shown enough frivolity; he tumbled Aubery to the ground by ducking his head from under his arm, and went to look for the meagre grazing. This water-hole was a poor one, unplanted and curiously deserted.

Most of the food they had been given was perishable, so they were more or less obliged to make a luxurious supper. As they prolonged the pleasure of sitting, full and sleepy and alone under the deep blue silent sky, Thomas speculated drowsily, 'But what do you think will happen to our knight? Will the lady marry him after all?'

'No,' said Brother James definitely. 'She had seen the foolishness of that before we left. She will marry the infidel chieftain and put the economy of Belle-Désirée on a sound basis. As for our knight, she is both wealthy and kind-hearted. She may send him with some of her people towards Jerusalem, or she may very well decide to keep him with her.'

'Keep him, when she's married to the infidel chieftain?'

'Did you notice that very pretty maid she had?' Aubery said with a grin. 'She was much more of an age for our knight.'

Brother James agreed with a stiff bend of his head. 'And if a strong party of Christians happened to pass by, the presence of a Christian knight would no doubt be valuable to her. No, I am much more concerned for his old war-horse.'

'He'll be all right,' said Aubery. 'The stable-boy told me. They'd marked him down to teach the boys to ride.'

As he fell asleep, Thomas realised that, while the donkey might very well have been ruthless about the knight, he would not have abandoned the old war-horse. In fact, as so often, he should have trusted the donkey.

All he had to worry about now was the landmarks for his home village. But he did wonder, as the days went on and still they came across no other travellers, why the ways should be so empty.

Presently they began to cross a succession of low sandy ridges that ran across their line of march. It made tiresome travelling, and especially to Thomas, because they obscured their destination. He counted them as they laboured across them; soon he would be able to see a long skyline with a double nick in it.

'What it's like, your village, Thomas?'

Breasting the slope eagerly, Thomas said, 'One well, but a good one, and we've led the water into streams through the gardens. Well planted, fourteen or fifteen huts–they may have built more since I was there–all with growing plots. And the trees–always seven trees at least. There were as many as twenty once, they say, and when I was a child—'

They topped the last crest, and Aubery said, 'You didn't say it was in the middle of a desert.'

'It's not a desert,' Thomas said crossly. 'You can't see it because it's getting dark.'

'Perhaps we should make camp,' said Brother James.

'Camp in sight of my mother's village? She'd never forgive us.' And Thomas started down the hill. Perhaps his sandal slid on the stony ground, so that he pulled too rudely on the halter; certainly there could be no other reason for the donkey to hang back.

An evening wind got up as they descended the slope, a squally chill little wind that blew first from one direction and then from another, though the sky above them remained clear and starry. It was all very silent, just as all the desert had been since they left Belle-Désirée. 'No path,' Brother James grunted as they jolted from shale to rock and back again.

'No need,' Thomas threw over his shoulder as he went down ahead of them in long joyous strides. 'In the rains it would get washed away. Why are you so slow?'

Here something gave way under his foot and he went head over heels and ended up against a boulder, laughing. The donkey, no doubt offended to have had his halter rudely twitched again, backed away. 'There,' said Thomas, limping back and rubbing his nose in apology, 'I'm sorry, I was clumsy. You pick the way.'

He looped the halter and put his hand on the saddle-bags to show his willingness to be guided. The donkey was slow to start, but moved off at last downhill, in the manner of donkeys seeming to turn this way and that at random but arriving very quickly at level ground. 'Left!' said Thomas jubilantly, for against the starry sky he could see the shape of the hills above his home.

The donkey put down his head and trudged.

They all trudged.

'I smell no water,' said Brother James.

Thomas looked up at the wheeling stars. 'A little farther yet.'

Aubery said, 'I'm tired. Couldn't we make camp now?'

'No,' said Brother James quietly; 'we must go on now.'

The donkey had not stopped trudging.

The stars wheeled farther. For the second time that night Thomas fell over something, and the donkey stood, its heavy head bowed.

'Why, it's wood,' said Thomas, as he knelt up in the sand. 'It's a–is it a tent-pole?'

But as he felt along the familiar shape there rose around him the smell of old burning.

'There are more here,' said Aubery, stooping to feel in the darkness.

'These are bones,' said Brother James.

The desert was silent.

They sat there until dawn. Brother James and Aubery huddled their blankets around them against the spiteful wind, but Thomas sat unmoving. Presently the donkey moved up to his back to shelter him.

Once he said, 'I should have known that the desert was too silent.'

When the light came they searched for whatever could be found.

It was not much. Aubery found a charred stake that might once have been a tree-stump, and Brother James found camel-droppings, but all of them had been washed by the rains and bleached by the sun. As for the bones, they had been burnt, and nothing could be made of them except for one skull with a fragment of steel embedded in it. The well had been choked with sand and stones, and without the tree-roots to hold the soil all the planted terraces had been washed away; not even Thomas could say where they had been.

Since there must be water somewhere under the surface, they scooped some holes and collected enough, brackish and swirling with sand, to last them a day, with care. They piled the burnt bones on a blanket, with the burnt wood as well, since they could not always tell which was which, and carried them to the edge of the valley, where there were loose stones they could roll into a tomb. They used their hands to shovel dry sand over them, and did what they could to wedge the stones so that they could not be moved. When they had finished, Brother James said a prayer over the pile. It did not seem to Thomas's stunned mind like any prayer for the dead that he had ever heard from any religion, but Brother James seemed sure of it, and in the circumstances it sounded acceptable.

'Father Almighty, maker of heaven and earth,' said Brother James in the circle of three bowed human heads and one bowed donkey's head: 'we have made this resting-place for our brothers, and if we are ignorant whether they were men or animals or trees we are persuaded that you made them all, and will accept our prayers for the eternal rest of them all. *Lux aeterna luceat eis, Domine; requiem aeternam dona eis, Domine. Amen.*'

'Amen,' said a white-faced Aubery; and in a small voice, 'Light eternal will be nice for trees.'

'Amen, amen. And rest eternal for animals,' said Brother James.

'Amen,' said Thomas voicelessly, to keep his mind from frantically counting. Who had been at home? His mother; old Yakoub; Uncle Simeon and his wife—

'I think now,' said Brother James, 'that we must make camp.

Thomas, the boy hasn't eaten since yesterday.'

'Yes,' said Thomas, trying to see Aubery's pinched face through the faces of his mother, his brothers, his sisters, Aunt Leah, her twins . . . 'Yes. Camp. Aubery, if you'll look for wood—' Surely his sisters had all married and left home? Surely not one of them had come back with her children—?

They found a boulder big enough to give them shade, and Aubery fell asleep with the last piece of bread in his hand. Brother James silently pulled his blanket over him, said his prayers with his head bowed towards the East, and rolled himself into his own blanket and lay still.

Thomas was left in the silence and heat of the day to count. His mother, Uncle Simeon's sons, surely he had been stupid to think that Peter would be at home—

They stayed there for the whole of that day. Brother James woke when the sun crept round to their side of the boulder, but Aubery did not move; Brother James picked him up, put him into the shade, and returned in silence to his own blanket. Thomas occupied himself with some tidying jobs until Brother James was asleep again, and then returned to his counting. There were so many who had retired since he left home. What about Aunt Dina, who had always said she would move in with them when her boys were grown? And there were the three orphaned cousins everyone had said must be looked after—

But not Peter. Peter could not have been at home.

And what had silenced the desert?

Thomas began again tidying the tidy camp.

It was at this camp in what had once been the Valley of the Seven Trees that the donkey first spoke to Thomas. There can be little doubt that he deliberately chose this moment; for neither then nor in later years did he show himself inclined to talk for the sake of talking, and in everyday matters they had already established sufficient communication. On the other hand, he never indulged in silence simply for the sake of mystification. All his communications, added up over the years, only confirmed what Thomas already knew: that the donkey understood the situation better than any of them.

He came up behind Thomas now, butted the back of his

shoulder, and said, 'How many miles to Jerusalem?'

Thomas recalled the days, which now seemed a lifetime past, when he had watered the abbey gardens and thought how companionable it would be to have a donkey to talk to. 'It's a comfort to have you, Ears,' he said absently, rubbing the long pale nose.

The donkey said coldly, 'My name is not Ears and I intended no comfort. My enquiry was practical. I understood that we were on Crusade.'

'We are,' said Thomas helplessly. 'Back to Antioch, was my contract, but perhaps Jerusalem too. By a very long way round, of course.'

'It is still measurable in miles,' said the donkey. 'How many?'

Thomas did not know. He had relied on his family for information.

'In a Traveller,' said the donkey offensively, 'I would call that irresponsible.'

He was quite right; but as he thought of the future Thomas felt the onset of panic. Behind him was Christendom, in front the unknown East; and he had accepted his contract.

'I am glad you have remembered that,' said the donkey. 'The situation is surely simple. You must go East. You know the landmarks?'

'Some; only some.'

'I see no reason for that to stop you,' said the donkey coldly. 'It has never, to my knowledge, stopped any other Traveller. The landmarks that you do not know you can discover. May I now go back to my rest? I remind you that you have so run down our stores that the next stages will be hard.'

'I am very sorry,' Thomas said humbly. 'I meant to buy them here.' He began to count again, not cousins but stores. 'Tomorrow won't be too bad, it won't be for a day or two that— There's a village over to the south where we might—'

But were all the villages silent now?

'And Ears! I mean, Brother Donkey. What about the boy? We can't take the boy with us.'

The donkey said with his eyes closed, 'What else can you do with him? Go to sleep.'

Abashed, Thomas did so.

When he woke, it was deep dusk and Brother James was nursing a pot over the fire and Aubery gathering wood.

'We need to leave this place,' said Brother James. 'We can march by night for a time.' Beside him lay a fire-blackened stave, which in the intervals of stirring the pot he was scraping and trimming. 'I had the fancy to take a staff from your home,' he said.

Aubery came back with an armful of wood. Somehow he seemed taller than Thomas remembered him, and quieter. There was about him something very like his brother Peter.

He said, 'Which way now, Thomas?'

'East,' said Thomas.

IX

It was desert country, sparse of water-holes and growing very little that even the donkey found eatable. It took all of Thomas's skill to find them spots where digging would yield a little pocket of water in the sand, and even when they discovered that Aubery was a dead shot with a sling there was not much to live off on the land. Even as late as the fifteenth day, Thomas was still taking the blame for the lack of food and water; but the next day, in some way he could not have explained, he began to look at the sandy ridges around with a measuring eye, and nod briefly to himself. On the eighteenth day he got up from breakfast and said calmly, 'Now somewhere on our left hand in a couple of hours' time—'

And just before noon they topped a ridge and saw below them a mile-wide valley, and strung along a great stretch of it a straggle of pack-camels and *meharis* and horses and donkeys and men on foot, all heading East.

They did not dare congratulate him; that would have meant that they had doubted him.

'We won't join it at once,' he decided. 'We'll carry on at this level until we see our chance to slip quietly in at the end.'

'Will we not be welcome?'

'Every peaceful traveller is welcome on a caravan. There must be a gift to the master, of course, but we might escape that.' He did not want to say that Thomas-ben-Matthias of the Guild, if he chose to make himself known, would not be asked for payment on any caravan.

'It all looks–well, peaceful,' said Aubery hesitating. 'Do you think they'll know anything about—'

They had not mentioned the Valley of the Seven Trees since they left it. Thomas said matter-of-factly, 'I don't think so. We've crossed to a different system of roads; and anyway, time has passed. They wouldn't be riding with so few armed men if there were any danger.'

During the day he noted some groups which stopped at the hour of prayer but did not unroll prayer-mats, and next afternoon, helped by a bend in the valley, they trotted down the slopes and swung in between two of these. A little later–it was a very well-run caravan–a horseman cantered down the line shouting at them not to straggle, and reined in beside them.

'*Salaam*, strangers. Just joined?'

'*Salaam*, adjutant. Thomas-ben-Matthias of the Guild. With a pilgrim and this boy. At your service.'

The adjutant saluted him. 'Welcome, Traveller. I'll remember you if we need help.'

It was almost a city life in the caravan. The merchants with spare stores travelled up near the centre. Thomas made his way there during the day, looked at prices, and in the evening sent Aubery up with instructions and some of their money. Aubery (who after all had grown up in city gutters) came back in triumph with some change. He had met some young people who needed music–did Thomas mind if he left them for a time? Brother James had been found by a man with a nasty rope-burn on his hand. Thomas recognised a son-in-law of a man who had known his father, and had a long and useful talk with him. Asked for news of his family, he said he had none recent, and turned the conversation to Eastern parts. To these people, Outremer was far in the West; but they seemed oddly ignorant of matters Easterly.

'I keep to the old familiar roads,' said his friend. 'I think you'll find that most of us prefer it like that nowadays: taking no risks. What risks there are I couldn't tell you, but when whole caravans go East and are never heard of again . . . No, it's not the

65

Khwarismians; out here we've always been on good terms with them. They've gone, anyway; I've no idea where; might have been wiped from the face of the world for all we've seen of them lately.'

'Could they have been,' said Thomas, casting his mind back to Miriam's youngest stepson, 'attacked from the East?'

His friend looked at him with a reluctant eye, and looked away again. 'How should I know? Everyone knows that the East stretches farther than any man has been, and holds things that no man has seen.'

Next day Thomas struck up an acquaintance with some pleasant but frivolous young men who knew the gossip around Baghdad. They were too close to it to put two and two together, but to Thomas it was clear that there was a silence in the East.

Padding along at the donkey's side, exchanging jokes and news, doing small favours in exchange for small favours, Thomas nosed through his fellow-travellers in search of someone who would know more. Within a couple of days he thought he had them.

It was a well-endowed party, ruled by a major-domo with a dozen servants and half a dozen maids, taking a rich widow home to Baghdad after a visit to a married daughter in Hama, and it was accompanied by two uncles of the widow's late husband, both of them rich merchants. Thomas helped with a refractory camel, made friends, accepted a gift of fruit, and in exchange asked permission to give them music after supper. Brother James, assured that the party was respectable even if infidel, consented to come to add a bass, and they even got Aubery to wash.

It was a thoroughly successful evening. The widowed lady made a gesture towards Muslim custom by remaining nominally in the shadows of her tent, but she beat time with a plump, ringed hand, hummed the refrains through her teeth, and was much taken by Aubery. He had too many urchin angularities to be a pretty boy, but he had lost his starved look, and his yellow hair and dark Eastern eyes gave him a wholly false air of pathos. It earned him a shower of almonds and sweetmeats from the widow, which he fairly put into his wallet to share later. Thomas was interested in the younger of the two uncles, and spent the evening moving gently in on him. This uncle, when he had complimented him on his singing, said, 'You are meaning to go East? Come and see me when we have a quieter evening. I think I could give you a warning.'

They got back to the donkey, tired and hoarse and loaded with gifts, and Thomas said, 'Tomorrow I may be able to tell you where we shall go next.'

But he never saw the younger uncle again, and by tomorrow had forgotten him and his warnings; for by then they had lost the donkey.

X

The broad valley which they had been following now bent into a region of broken ridges, which everyone agreed looked likely to harbour bandits, and a horseman rode back with orders from the master of the caravan to close up for defence. The widow's big party was sent to the centre for safety, the smaller parties on foot put in front of those who were mounted, and Thomas hailed to know if he were the Traveller.

'Thomas-ben-Matthias. With the pilgrim and this boy.'

The horseman saluted Brother James with respect. 'Be so good as to move to safety with the centre, reverend sir. Traveller, may I have your boy to help with the horses? And there's a camel broken down quarter of a mile on the left, holding us up; will you and your donkey deal with that? The rest of you, close up and stop ambling. There's a troop of *meharis* falling back to ride herd on you.'

Thomas took the donkey forward at a trot. It was not the camel that had broken down but its load, which was around its feet, with every other camel in the neighbourhood proclaiming its determination not to take one ounce more. He prudently made himself responsible for one bale that would not disagree with his donkey, saw the rest of it re-packed, and jogged on with them. Presently he found himself talking to the owner of the camels.

The difficult bales, he said, were a consignment of very rare silks he was taking to Baghdad. He was old to be on the roads, and after a time began a long grumble about the band of undutiful sons who had made this necessary. One was lazy, and would rather sit at home than go out after an honest profit; a second was a fool; and worst of all was the third, who if he did not mend his ways would be turned out without a penny to go and find this king, which was all he ever thought about.

'Eh?' said Thomas, jarred from the nodding half-attention he had been giving the old man. 'What king? Where?'

'Trinkets!' said the old man scornfully. 'Petty worked pieces of silver; and against the law of the Prophet at that, being images of a human head.'

'Where did they come from?'

'How should I know? Somewhere South or South-East, and he paid good money to own them, the young fool, and now all he wants to do is to go where *he* went: the greatest king who ever lived, he said.'

'Do you . . .' said Thomas hesitatingly, 'do you remember his name?'

'No,' said the old man perversely. 'What have I to do with kings who steal away my fine sons? Anyway he's long dead, I heard that somewhere. My curses on him for my son, my curses on that Iskander.'

Thomas was disappointed; in no way could he see that Iskander could be mistaken for John. But after a time he began to think further. The desert was full of tales about kings and heroes, and nearly all of them had some shred of truth somewhere. Prester John's kingdom was old. It had been founded by Saint Thomas; why should it not have been strengthened by an Iskander, and then descended to a John?

When they off-loaded in the evening, he said to the donkey, 'You won't mind if I leave you for an hour?' The donkey merely backed away crossly, because by the rule of the caravan he was hobbled. Thomas pocketed the good piece of cheese the old man had given him and went in search of his companions. Aubery was busy and boastful among the horses, and waved that he did not need food. Brother James was in the more surprising setting of a noisy family party, very much petted and deferred to.

'There was a child feverish,' he explained, taking Thomas to a quieter spot. 'No, I need neither food nor lodging, I thank you.'

Between mouthfuls of cheese Thomas explained his problem about Iskander, and Brother James considered it.

'This Iskander I take to be Alexander the Greek: a great king admired by all Franks.'

'Not a Greek, then. Franks think Greeks weak and heretical.'

'A different kind of Greek: long ago. Your informant said he was dead. He was a great traveller, but he never reached Cathay. He went to the Indies and back, and died at Susa.'

'Could he have been converted by the Apostle Thomas first?'

This seemed to Thomas a solution that fitted the facts, but Brother James shook his head decidedly. 'Iskander was long before the Apostle's time.'

Thomas found this confusing. In the abbey he had been taught that nothing of importance had happened before the birth of Christ. This had seemed good sense then, for how could anything be of importance when everyone taking part was automatically damned? 'Well then—could he have established a kingdom that the Apostle converted and Prester John inherited?'

Brother James said nothing. Thomas finished his cheese. 'We'll stay with this caravan as far as Baghdad. If you think we should turn South, it must be then. Will you think about that, please?'

The grateful family pressed on him some dried fruits, and enjoyably munching these he padded back through noisy arguments, smells of cooking, shifting and snorting of baggage beasts, stray drifts of music. He kept a piece of fruit for his donkey, and was so anxious to give him this unexpected treat to make up for the indignity of the hobble that he ran the last stretch.

He ran into chaos. His donkey was gone. So was the donkey's load; so was the bale he had been carrying for the old camel-owner. So were three of the camel-owner's camels, with the whole of the consignment of very rare silk.

XI

The theft of four baggage-animals and their loads being a disgrace in a well-run caravan, an outcry was raised and a runner sent to the master. Soon an adjutant arrived with his scimitar in his belt and began questioning. A few disregarded objects were found and returned to Thomas: an old blanket, a cup that had rolled away. He could hardly pull himself together to take them, in the face of what he had lost: all their goods but for what they carried in their wallets, the donkey's harness with the diamond, and the donkey himself, his donkey, his donkey! To the adjutant he could only say distractedly, 'My donkey, I've lost everything, I've lost my donkey!'

A man from the crowd had meanwhile thrust himself into the torchlight to ask, 'Did anyone see a man with two fingers missing on his left hand and a gouged scar on his cheek?'

Half a dozen voices clamoured that they had; that man and three others had come from nowhere to help when the camel had broken down.

'The usual trick. They probably cut the girth. That man lifted two prize *meharis* from the Mecca caravan three years ago.'

There was a long and noisy argument about his blame in not having said so before. Thomas, sitting on the ground with his head in his hands, said only, 'I don't know, I didn't see him. What's happened to my donkey? It was my fault, I hobbled him. No one could have stolen my donkey if he wasn't hobbled.'

'The situation is clear,' the adjutant pronounced at last. 'This camel-owner and this Traveller have both suffered losses, and compensation will be paid. This man did not report the presence of a thief, and will give the Traveller food and shelter for tonight.'

The camel-owner thanked him effusively, the man who had seen the thieves protested that he would have offered food and shelter anyway out of charity, and Thomas made shift to utter the proper words. Everyone simmered down and slept. Thomas alone stayed awake, staring into the dark. He had lost everything; he had lost his donkey.

In the morning his neighbours said, 'Can we lend you any-thing, friend? Aren't you ready?' Thomas did not move.

The caravan got under way, group by group moving up to the low skyline ahead and jogging over and below it. When nothing remained to be seen and the last clatter and chatter had faded from the morning air, Thomas got up, slung over his shoulder the only blanket remaining to him, and began to trudge towards the highest point he could see.

It was his fault. He had hobbled his donkey. He could only hope that his donkey was forgiving enough to have left him signs of its passing. He had absolutely no doubt that if the donkey wanted to he would find a way.

The first thing he saw from his high point was two figures climbing the same slope. As they laboured up to him Aubery said without greeting, 'Which way, do you think, Thomas?'

Thomas looked around him at the land of cold blue distances and cold grey ridges, while the wind stung his eyes into tears. 'Not South, or they would have had to pass through the caravan. Nor West, or we could see their tracks from here.'

Not many directions were possible. 'North, then,' said Aubery. 'We'll keep to the high ground.'

Brother James said to Thomas, 'We saw the caravan-master. He gave us compensation in food and blankets. Why did they take the donkey?'

'To carry a stolen bale of silk.'

'Not because they knew of the diamond?'

'I don't think so.'

They went North all day. They were on the right trail, for the reason that there were no other trails. The light was nearly gone when Aubery's sharp eyes saw something ahead that was not a stone. When they had laboured up to it, they found that it was the donkey's saddle-pad, which Thomas had made from scraps of leather and blanket to stop the girth rubbing.

'They dropped it?'

Thomas burst out, 'Of course not! They didn't off-load here. The donkey rubbed it off. He meant it to guide us. It's all right now, we can follow him, he'll go on guiding us. Come on!'

There were few days after that when they did not find some clue left by the donkey. This became day by day more necessary, and in more ways than one. Not only were there side-valleys where the thieves might have turned off, but also this high bare land offered little in the way of fuel for the fire, and donkey-dung, dried by the bitter winds, burnt well. He left them hoof-prints now and again as well, and once a piece of blue cloth torn from a pair of breeches.

'Yes, well,' said Aubery when Thomas came up proudly to show them this: 'if he's taking such care of us, why doesn't he escape?'

'We can see from the hoof-prints,' Brother James said reasonably, 'that he is hobbled at night.'

'He's not hobbled in the day. And there are four men and three camels; they can't keep an eye on him all the time.'

'No,' said Thomas, 'you're wrong, Aubery. I have thought about this. He doesn't know how far we are behind him. If he escaped now and turned back to us, one of the thieves could overtake him on a camel; and if he still found his way back to us how would we feed him? He knows that we can't carry food for all four of us without him, and there's not enough grazing here to take him back to the caravan camp. No, you don't have to worry; the donkey understands the situation better than we do.'

'I hadn't thought of the fodder,' Aubery admitted. 'But where are we going, Thomas? Do *you* know?'

'Not yet.'

'How do you mean?'

'Well.' Thomas collected his thoughts to explain what to him was obvious. 'This is only a little local trail. When it arrives wherever it's going I shall see some landmarks, or pick up a name I've heard of, or—' He gave up the effort to describe the hundred small details of weather and trees and language and clothes which together fixed for him his position on the map he had carried in his head, expanding it and adding detail to it, ever since he was a small child. 'Don't worry; I shall find out.'

That night, huddled around their precious fire–it was too precious, in the chill of these ranges, for their old careless method of making camp, and the moment the first spark was kindled all three of them pulled their blankets round their shoulders and crouched over the warmth–that night, as he nursed the bowl of tisane over the embers, Brother James said meditatively, 'And yet it comes to me that but for the donkey we might now be on our way South.'

'It would be warmer.' Aubery sighed.

'But wrong.'

'You've made up your mind then?' said Thomas, holding their cups ready so that none of the warmth would be wasted.

'I have consulted my memory,' said Brother James, his stately manner not in the least diminished by the way he was juggling the hot bowl to pour the tisane without scalding his fingers, 'and called to mind that the kingdom of Iskander was some three hundred years before the birth of Christ. That, I think, is altogether too long ago for his kingdom to be the same as Prester John's.'

'Were there kingdoms before Christ?' Aubery asked, taking his cup and wrapping his hands round it with a shiver. 'Well, don't look at me like that, Brother James! I never had any schooling.'

'Your knowledge of the Gospels,' Brother James said severely, 'should have informed you of the Romans. There were many others.'

'They tell you about them,' Thomas put in between sips, moving his cup so that the steam warmed his nose and cheeks. 'Travel through Persia and they'll tell you of their kingdom that was never defeated.'

'It was defeated by the Greeks,' said Brother James through his little veil of steam.

'Well, don't tell a Persian so.'

'By Alexander the Greek?' Aubery enquired.

'By other Greeks before Alexander too: a different kind of Greek.'

'Different from the kind nowadays?'

'Quite different.'

'They must have been very long ago,' said Aubery, impressed.

Thomas shook his head. 'The Egyptians sneer at *any* kingdom as upstart. They say theirs was before all kingdoms, and the greatest and the longest-lasting. They were probably different Egyptians too. I didn't know you were learned in these matters, Brother James.'

'I have read where I could,' said Brother James. 'Even before I had heard of Prester John I enquired in every library and scriptorium of the West for writings about distant places.' He shook his head sadly. 'I fear there was much written in a spirit of vanity. I will not say that deception was intended, but on many occasions it was achieved.'

'But your travels were all in the West.'

'Yes. I had intended the pilgrimage to Jerusalem, of course, but there were other lands to be seen first. . . . My father,' said Brother James after a ruminative pause, making Thomas blink, for he could not imagine Brother James with a father: 'my father travelled to Byzantium as a young man. I only remember him weary and ailing, for they have pestilent fevers there which never leave you, but in his time he must have been a bold traveller. He brought home with him many choice outlandish things, in particular one . . . Well,' said Brother James creakily, 'I will show it to you. I have carried it over most of Christendom without taking it from my wallet, but since we are on our way East–eventually, that is to say–it may be a piece of valuable knowledge.'

He carefully drank the last drops of the tisane and opened his wallet. From it he took a finger-length roll of soft leather. Inside it was a piece of ivory silk, raw-edged as if it had been cut from a larger piece. He laid a corner of his blanket on the ground and held open the silk on it.

'A monster!' Aubery gasped.

It was silk embroidery, but one did not notice the stitches. The monster floated on the ivory ground, its fringed paws and tail displayed. Feathered, scaled?–impossible to be sure. Its open mouth and round eyballs were scarlet, as were its strong curved claws. Its expression was imperious and relishing, with a certain jollity imparted by its plump cheek and chops.

'A dragon,' said Brother James, carefully re-rolling the silk. 'Such are to be found, according to my father, in Cathay. Even as a young child I harboured the wish to go to Cathay and see dragons.'

It was a day or two after this–or perhaps more than a day or two, for the days were so much alike it was difficult to tell one from another–that Thomas was shamed. During that day, something had occurred under his feet. Nothing seemed to have altered in the sky or on the skylines, but under his feet the land said, at first tentatively and then definitely, Down.

'I think,' he said at supper (the same tisane, the same dry barley biscuit, a morsel of date to give warmth in the bitter bright night), 'I think we have crossed the top of this country. Soon we shall be going downhill fast.'

He was so certain that they had to believe him, and Aubery said, 'After so long! How long, Thomas?'

And Thomas had forgotten his tally-stick.

It had been lost, of course, with the rest of their goods in the donkey's saddle-bags; but he had never thought to start another. The tally-stick is one of the tools of the Traveller. And up here there was nothing fit to make a new one: no more than the wind-dried skeletons of old grasses.

It took him some time to recover from his shame. Aubery, surprisingly kindly, said to him, 'The old one was almost finished. Start a new one from the day we left the caravan.'

Brother James said, 'You could use my staff.'

It was the staff he had brought from the Valley of the Seven Trees, blackened by fire until it was as hard as iron. Thomas could not take his knife to it. He said foolishly, 'It will weaken it if I cut it. There must be something else we can use.'

In the end they unravelled three threads from Thomas's blanket, plaited them together, and marked the days by knots. This proved even more shaming; for Thomas could not remember how many days had passed without the donkey, and had to ask for help. Brother James's estimate was fifteen, but made doubtfully. Thomas might have agreed with that, but Aubery asserted it was at least thirty. When Thomas refused to believe this, he broke out passionately, 'Half my life-time, then!'

'Nonsense . . . How old are you, though?'

'How should I know? In Outremer I think I was twelve,' said Aubery crossly.

A couple of days later, when Brother James had been thundering at Aubery for scamping his morning prayers, another piece of forgetfulness came into Thomas's shocked mind.

'Brother James—we never kept Christmas!'

'Christmas?' said Brother James, and for once looked quite blank. 'Have we missed it?'

'I don't know.'

'We can't have missed it. Christmas is the depth of winter.'

Thomas looked helplessly around. Nothing grew on the stone-grey lands that would tell them the time of year. 'Do you think it would be displeasing to heaven to celebrate Christmas at the wrong time?'

'It would be worse, I think, not to celebrate it at all.'

'Yes. We will celebrate Christmas,' said Thomas with the certainty of inspiration, 'when we find my donkey.'

As he had promised, the trail began now to lead down into less barren parts, trees began to appear and a thin stringy grass, and one day a curious cluster of earthy mounds, which as they came closer resolved themselves into the roofs of a tiny village.

Brother James and Aubery at once took fright–a phenomenon well known among those who went long without seeing people–and proposed skirting it. Professionally scornful, Thomas marched them into the village street. The villagers were almost equally shy, tending to stand stock-still and pretend they were not there when they were addressed, and it was some time before Thomas could get from them a word of greeting to tell him what language they spoke. It proved to be a kind of Turkish with many Arabic words in it, and presently the headman pointed at Brother James and appeared to ask, 'Is your wise man a wise man?'

'Yes, he is; very wise. Who is sick?'

It was the headman's wife. Brother James mixed her a feverfew and looked at two more wives and a line of children, and Aubery, suddenly becoming himself again, taught six more children a dancing game, got out his pipe for the first time for weeks, and learnt some very informal words of greeting. Thomas did even better. They wove good blankets there, and when he asked to buy three they were pressed on him in payment, and he was able to ask what other travellers had passed this way.

He was quietly triumphant as they left the village. 'The donkey is only a day ahead of us.'

'So that's why you wouldn't sleep there,' said Aubery, who in the end had been a little wistful at leaving. 'Right; we can step out. And here's something to help us.' With a wicked grin he produced a slab of some confection made of honey and almonds.

'Begging,' said Thomas in disgust; that was beneath the dignity of a Traveller.

'I was not. They have an old blind piper there and I taught him five new songs.'

It was good stuff to march on. That night, with the donkey so near ahead of them, they did not stop to camp until it was too dark to see their steps, and by then it was too cold to fumble with lighting a fire; they huddled in their blankets and ate the honey-cake, and found it as good as a full meal.

'Tomorrow,' said Thomas, 'we shall find the donkey.'

On the three curled-up figures close together under the wide and starry sky there fell a silence. Then Aubery said in a voice smaller than usual, 'Thomas: what shall we do then?'

He added carelessly after a time, 'Of course there are only four of them, and I have my sling.'

'We are men of peace,' Brother James said austerely.

'But they aren't. And anyway,' Aubery corrected him, 'we aren't either; we are Crusaders.'

This might have led to argument, but it was too cold. Thomas in fact had never had any plan for the recovery of his donkey; he had always known that this was not necessary.

They had arrived now at the end of the plateau they had been travelling for so many weeks; here it broke down into a great green jumbled valley, full of lacy streams and white waterfalls and dense evergreen forests, a most grateful sight after the stony wastes above. But what was not grateful was the way the main valley had half a dozen smaller ones leading from it, wooded ghylls in which a travelling party could hide for days. And there was such a travelling party below them: an assembly of dots that resolved itself into a tent, four men, three camels, and one donkey.

For the first few minutes after this sighting of his donkey, Thomas was not very useful; he could only look down at it in blissful content. When they had persuaded him to consider the situation more constructively, he took one look around, said, 'We must catch them at once,' and plunged downward.

'But Thomas!'

'Come *on*.'

They were seen before they had gone very far, for it was hard

77

going on the rocky slopes; but it seemed that the thieves had not thought that they were still pursued, for they were making a leisurely stop in this first comfortable camp and letting their animals graze. The camels were appreciating it, and it is never easy to take a camel from what it appreciates. By the time Thomas was on level ground the thieves had given up the attempt to strike camp and were waiting for them.

'What will we *do*?' Aubery gasped from behind; but Thomas pressed grimly on.

The leader came forward as the Crusaders neared them, the man with the missing fingers and the scar on his cheek-bone. He had a good look at what was threatening him, and laughed.

'You appear to me,' he announced in kitchen-Arabic, 'to be the most shameless kind of brigands. I must inform you that we are all armed, but we will refrain from taking action against you provided that you sheer off at once.'

'I want my donkey,' said Thomas, and advanced upon him.

The leader brought up his knife.

'Get out of the way of my donkey!' said Thomas, and passionately wiped him aside. Wrong-footed, the leader went over backwards on to hard ground and dropped his knife.

'We need that donkey!' said the second man, and ran at Thomas. Brother James, that man of peace, did not strike at him with his staff; he merely brought it up level so that the man ran damagingly into it and collapsed winded. At the same moment the stone from Aubery's sling caught the leader even more damagingly just below the eye.

'Two and a boy against us!' said the third man derisively to the fourth. They took their time about it, each getting a cudgel from their belongings and one even producing a scimitar. The donkey surveyed the field of battle, trotted into the middle of it, and slapped both hind hooves into the stomach of the biggest man. Then he nodded at Thomas to follow and cantered gently off up one of the smaller valleys.

That night they celebrated Christmas Eve.

It was a brief celebration, for the battle had been tiring, and soon after Brother James had said an especially long grace Aubery dropped asleep. Brother James covered him up, saying,

'We are on Crusade, and it will be forgiven us if we make our prayers only as we can. I am an old man and will make mine here.'

Thomas built up the fire, took an extra-large piece of bread, put his blanket round his shoulders, and climbed up through the trees to find his donkey. He was cropping the grass just above the tree-line, at the foot of the bare slope that led to the star-filled sky.

'Here's your bread. Oh Ears, you're back with us, oh *Ears!*' said Thomas, putting one arm round the strong neck.

The donkey ate the bread. 'Since it's Christmas,' he said, though distantly, 'for once you may call me that. I had expected you a day or so sooner, but I'm glad to be back. They hobbled me at night, and the camels had no conversation.'

'But Ears, we're months out of our way,' Thomas said wretchedly, 'and it was all my fault.'

The donkey snatched a mouthful of grass. 'There is no need to be extravagant,' he said munching. 'If no worse than this happens to us, we shall be lucky. As for being out of our way, it is news to me that we have a way to be out of. As I understood it, our business is to search Asia; which, I remind you, we have hardly yet begun to do. This is excellent grass.' He ate some more of it.

Thomas watched him lovingly. 'The others are asleep. I came up to you, Ears, because it's Christmas Eve and nearly midnight. We must make our Christmas prayers.'

The donkey turned his heavy head to look at him. 'What has led you to assume that I am a Christian?' he enquired coldly.

Shocked, Thomas gaped at him. '*You*, Ears, not a Christian? But–but all donkeys are Christian! You carried Christ into Jerusalem!'

'Possibly. We will carry anyone anywhere. To carry people is our business in life. We take pride in doing it well.'

'But you're on Crusade!'

'I am making a journey,' the donkey corrected him. 'This is my business. As it is yours.'

'*I* am on Crusade,' Thomas protested.

'Possibly. You *may* be passionately concerned to rescue the Holy City from such as your brother-in-law Hakim (who is an estimable man and understands donkeys). If so, I have seen no sign of it. You appear to me to be a Traveller carrying out his business in life.'

'Like a donkey?' Thomas said feebly.

The donkey looked him over. 'You think it a light matter to be a donkey?' he enquired.

'No,' said Thomas. 'Most certainly not. I would regard it as an honour to be a donkey, Ears.'

'Among donkeys,' said the donkey, 'the Traveller is recognised as an allied breed. We donkeys do our work, require nothing beyond our daily fodder, and take pride in our kind. Few achieve so much. As for this matter of my religion, if it were not that I had come to have a certain amount of trust in you, I would find your attitude offensive. You have your faith and I have mine, and that is enough for both of us. If more men followed the example of the donkeys, in this as in other matters, the world would be a better place to live in.'

'I beg your pardon, Ears,' said Thomas humbly, and started off to his lonely prayers.

'However,' said the donkey, softening slightly, 'I have no objection to telling you that I too celebrate the last day of the year. You are some days out in your reckoning, but better a late celebration than none at all. We will celebrate the day together.'

So Thomas and his donkey climbed above the trees to look at the stars above the mountains, and each celebrated in silence what was in their natures to celebrate.

XII

They had of course made certain at once that the diamond was still in the donkey's girth, but curiously enough it had not occurred to them to wonder what the thieves had packed into the saddle-bags. It proved to be a very fair supply of food; and that was as well, for after a couple of days in the pleasant valley the land rose again and they were labouring in snow.

Aubery had barely heard of snow before, and declared that it was not possible. After a long time Brother James said, 'I threw snowballs as a boy,' which seemed even less possible. Aubery had not thought of snowballs, and for a day or two ran riot, inventing a great many similar games, which Brother James admitted to having played also. He seemed to find a gaunt pleasure in the memories.

'Is your home like this, then?' Aubery asked, rubbing his wet hands on his sides and flapping his arms to keep warm.

'No.'

'Like what, then?'

After an even longer pause Brother James said, 'Small. Green,' and then no more.

But quite soon even Aubery gave up regarding snow as fit for games. Snow killed the tips of the fingers, blackened the ears, and reduced the traveller to a state of mindless monotonous blankness that argued a close co-operation with demons. There were no landmarks here except those provided by a Traveller's sense of how the mountains grew. Thomas watched them incessantly, making out slowly how their spines lay, where their flanks were folded in to them, how the windings of the small streams between them gave a clue to the lie of the next ridge they must fight their way over. When Aubery enquired, 'But Thomas, where are we going now?' he could answer with no hesitation, 'The only way possible.'

This way led them, just before their food was finished, to a very odd village whose houses seemed to be cut from solid ice. The people said they had warm summers, so presumably there was something solid behind the ice, but it was not visible. They were a friendly people, welcoming the Crusade with not the least thought of any advantage they might get from it. When Brother James cured some of their sick, they were as much surprised as grateful.

Another odd thing about the village was that it had neither church nor mosque. What it did have they discovered only on the day they left, when the three brawny young men who had promised to put them on their way insisted on taking them ceremoniously into a deep chamber in the ice where lamps burnt valuable oil for no apparent reason in front of some ordinary pieces of stone. Here they knelt down, prepared and lit more lamps, and began a recitation.

Thomas was in time to murmur, 'Hush,' and they survived the visit without giving offence. It was not until they were outside that realisation dawned on Aubery. 'They're *idolaters!*'

'Hush.'

'It appears,' said Brother James, grim but at least tactful enough to speak in Frankish, 'that we have been deceived into attending a pagan ceremony of worship.'

'We weren't asked to worship.'

'No. And they are good people. They have the Christian virtues. We must hope that they will find religious instruction soon.'

'I know some Christians who could do with idolatrous virtues,' Aubery said; and Brother James for once did not thunder at him.

Once they were ready to leave Thomas thought it worth while to see if the name of Christian meant anything to them.

'Keriss'n?' said the headman: 'no, I don't think we— Oh, you mean *that* lot?' He sketched a cross in the air, and pointed North.

Thomas pointed West.

'No, no,' said the headman. 'We know about them in the West, but they're not real Keriss'ns. Don't you let them deceive you. The only real Keriss'ns are the ones in the North, and they've told us about the false ones. The false ones are Rettical.'

Thomas tried to work this out. 'You know the ones in the North well?'

'Only in the summer. A long way and useless. They have a city. Ornamental, but—' He made a wry face. 'Not for civilised people like us. Near to the—' He had no word for this, and made motions with his flattened hand and spat. 'Useless; bad-tasting.'

'Sea,' said Thomas, calculating. 'Trebizond?'

The headman corrected his pronunciation, but agreed: Trebizond. 'You think of going there? Nice people, but with barbarous habits: buildings, both above ground and on the–what was that word?'

'Sea. What was that other word?'

'Rettical. What those pretended Keriss'ns in the West are.'

'What is this?' Brother James asked.

Thomas laughed. 'Heretical.'

'Eh?'

Thomas said carefully, 'The word is an uncivilised exclamation of disapproval. Can you give me the landmarks for Trebizond?'

'For a short way. We are not Travellers, and only two or three of us go out of civilised lands. Will that be enough?'

'Quite enough. And we thank you for your unbounded hospitality and we should be on our way now.'

'Travel will be easier soon,' said the good idolatrous people, filling their bags and pummelling them to get more in. 'Spring is coming!'

The three young men set them on their way and gave them some useful pieces of advice. These included a warning against a very prevalent type of snow-demon, who had seven toes on each foot and could be kept off only by means of a magic sign with the hand; a surprising way of defeating the cold by burrowing into the coldest thing around, a snow-drift; and a business-like way of preserving the evening fire by baking a small pot of clay and sealing a piece of charcoal into it. When they said their final goodbyes, Aubery asked doubtfully, 'You did say it was spring?'

'Can't you see that the snow is melting?' said the brawny young men.

'But why should we be going North to Trebizond?' Brother James asked restively. 'Our way should be East.'

'I'd like to see a city again,' said Aubery, dazzled.

'This land is all mountains,' said Thomas, 'and hard travelling Easterly. But Trebizond is one of the gathering-points for the caravans on the Easterly roads. We shall save time if we join a caravan there.'

'But they couldn't give you directions beyond two days' march. Can you find Trebizond?'

'I can find Trebizond,' said Thomas with professional scorn. 'And they did say that the snows are melting.'

They were melting. While no less cold, they had become more drenching, and developed the habit of gathering in a solid-seeming floor over icy torrents beneath. It was a miserable time; Aubery, who had left the village expecting flowery meadows and a splendid city, wept with exasperation.

On the worst day of all, Thomas lost them. Floundering down a mile-wide ravine in a storm of scudding sleet, he found that he was alone with the donkey, and could only plunge horridly on and trust that they would keep the direction. Soon the sleet began to turn into a dense white mist which by contrast looked almost restful, and out of this mist came a tranquil creature who smiled in a way that turned the mist to warm gold and offered the answer to all problems if Thomas would only lie down and listen. How many toes it had was not in question, since it did not appear even to have feet, drifting gracefully over the ground in a way that Thomas understood he could do himself so long as he followed it closely. It was all but on him before he recalled himself enough to cry, 'Ears, oh Ears!' The donkey occurred right in the middle of the creature, but the slap of its two hind hooves had the usual satisfactory result. The creature vanished, Thomas found himself clutching a rock in the middle of a torrent, and the donkey waded out to him and gave him a shoulder to get him to the bank.

'Ears!' said Thomas, getting his feet on firm land and collapsing in tears on to the strong grey shoulder.

'My name is not Ears,' said the donkey coldly, 'and our friends are quite two miles away and very frightened to have lost us. Hadn't you better pull yourself together?'

They found the other two, and Thomas was pleasantly firm with them about the necessity of following the guide closely; and they went on in the direction of Trebizond.

XIII

'Look!' said Aubery one morning. 'We're coming to cultivated land. Are we near this city?'

They had wound their way down from the mountains, through pine-forests and leafy forests and marshy forests, and now they were in pleasant little foothills, with water-courses overgrown with ferns and cresses. Their path was jolting down to flat lands of red earth all washed over with green.

To Aubery's annoyance, Thomas at once abandoned this path

to look for a point of vantage whence he could see the ways of the plain.

'But I want to see the city!' Aubery complained.

'There it is,' Thomas said nodding. The plain ran away in green mist, until at the horizon the mist turned to a shadowy blue, with points in it here and there that might have been gold if they were brighter, and thickenings that might have been grey if they were darker. 'The morning mist is hiding it. They say,' he added, 'that there is no lovelier city than Trebizond in all the world.'

'Then let us come to it!' said Aubery, hopping from foot to foot with impatience.

'Wait!' said Thomas, and marked their way. Into the spring fields ran a long crescent of woodland; they would follow the edge of that, cut across to a broad belt of orchards in dazzling white bloom—and what was that chequer-board look beyond the orchards?

'The out-fields of the city, I think,' said Brother James, standing with his thorny beard blowing in the warm wind. 'A pleasant sight, Thomas.'

'Little gardens and allotments,' Thomas agreed. 'Well, they will be frequented at this time of year. We can stop there and ask directions.'

'Where shall we sleep?' Aubery asked round-eyed. He had grown used to camping on what spot they chose.

'If they are Christians,' said Brother James austerely, as they returned to their path, 'they will have houses of charity for the use of pilgrims.' He pondered. 'Though they are heretical: I had forgotten. Thomas, do heretics have houses of charity?'

'Yes. But I would rather find a house of Travellers.'

'Why?' Aubery demanded. He had been growing a little tiresome in this way recently, demanding to be given reasons for every smallest action.

Thomas said after a pause, 'We need to know if there is a caravan going out soon.' In fact he was not sure why he wanted to be with his own people in Trebizond. Perhaps it was because they had been so long solitary—this affected even seasoned Travellers—that he was shy of crowds. Perhaps, perhaps. But somehow his steps were lagging behind the others'.

85

And yet, as he looked over the green and blue plain, with its swathes of woodland, and at the point where the green turned into blue with a certain translucency in the air that meant the sea beyond–suddenly he thought that somewhere there might be the wells and gardens and friendly huts that he had lost in the Valley of the Seven Trees.

But, to his alarm, he found as they walked that Brother James and Aubery were slightly ahead, while the donkey was plodding well behind them.

'I don't understand about heretics,' Aubery observed as they struck into the shade of the crescent of woodland. The broad fields of rich red earth needed no irrigation beyond the little natural streams that meandered through them; there was no one to be seen. 'I know people used to say–when I was a child–*heretic*, as they said *murderer* and *thief*. But I never understood what they had *done*.'

Thomas left this one to Brother James; who after a time said, 'What may be proper in Christendom is not so out of Christendom. Regard them as you would Muslims and idolaters, Aubery. If they are good people, that suffices.'

Aubery, naturally, was ready to argue this; he, but not Thomas, thought it was by chance that the donkey came up behind him and bunted him in the back; so that there was an interval before Aubery resumed, 'Yes, but I don't understand why there is this Christian city and you call it out of Christendom. And why do we have to walk all round this bit of woodland when there's a much straighter way through these fields?'

Brother James left that one to Thomas. To discourage Aubery, Thomas said, 'There's a lot of history behind it,' and Aubery said passionately, 'Don't try to *teach* me!' Brother James had been worrying a little about his education lately.

'I won't,' Thomas said peaceably. 'Trebizond was a great trading city long before even the memory of my Guild, because the roads from the East meet here and it has a good harbour. Its people are of the Greek rite, and the Franks hate the Greek rite.'

'They hate them,' struck in Aubery, showing off his knowledge, 'more than they hate the Muslims. They fight them–don't they?'

Brother James murmured something sorrowful. Thomas said,

'They have fought them, yes. You don't want a history lesson—no, all right; but fifty years ago the Franks treacherously attacked the Greeks—'

'Well, we're all Christians,' Aubery said sunnily. 'Straight on through these orchards? Peace be on you, brother!'

They had been talking in Frankish, and as the native of Trebizond ducked under the blossom of the boughs towards them he gaily greeted him in Frankish.

Thomas grasped his arm hard to stop him, and repeated the greeting in Greek, with the age-old sign of the empty palms.

The native of Trebizond stared. He was a lean middle-aged man in a blue tunic, carrying a hoe under his arm, and over his shoulder a bundle that held his dinner. His belt also held a knife, on which he put his hand.

Thomas still held his hands open. He said in Greek, 'Peace to all in these lands. We are peaceful travellers. May we come within the city?'

The native of Trebizond shifted his hoe into his other hand. He fell back a step.

Thomas said, 'We are three and a donkey. We come only for shelter. May we enter the city?'

The native of Trebizond fell back farther, backing into the blossom.

'Is this the way to the city gate?' Thomas asked desperately.

The native of Trebizond pointed hurriedly with the hoe, ducked under the blossom, and disappeared. They heard his footsteps padding on the soft ground.

'On!' said Thomas, and gathered the donkey's halter and led the way.

'Well!' said Aubery, critical of bad manners.

They made their way in silence to the farther edge of the orchard. It was not yet noon, but after a look around Thomas said, 'We'll camp here. Aubery, see to the donkey, please.'

'Where are you going?'

'There's a little hill over there. I want to see the city.'

And then a strange and disturbing thing happened. The donkey sombrely watched Thomas go, and put back his ears and stretched out his neck and uttered his wild and terrifying cry of warning.

'Take care—take care—take care!'

Steadily Thomas climbed the hill until he found a spot with a view.

The morning mists had cleared. As he looked at the city of Trebizond, high on its cliffs overlooking the sea, he was struck by a feeling he thought no Traveller could ever admit. He longed to enter that city. Beyond the small gardens and allotments in the out-fields rose the strong walls, with the turreted barbican over the open gates. Within the walls the stone houses rose street by street, all interlaced with tree-lined paths and climbing alleys and steep twisting stairways. Shining above them all were the slender towers of the citadel, on the East silver-gold in the sun, on the West blue-gold in the shade, and below and beyond them all lay the calm levels and gold-pricked waves of the sea.

And as he searched the nearer ground he saw what he had feared he might see. In the clear air he could make out the blue tunic, and the dinner-bag bumping on the man's shoulder in his panic-stricken speed. He had run hard to make the circuit through the orchards and still outstrip them. Thomas saw the blue dot race into the allotments, and a tiny movement as an arm waved, and then every allotment began to boil with movement. More blue dots, and brown and green and red dots, made at speed for the gate. He saw them converge and be gathered into their city; he heard the dull clang as the great gate closed after them, and the high clear notes of the battle-trumpets; and he watched, until the sight was blurred by tears, the shining arms of the defenders of Trebizond, mustering on the gate against the enemy Crusaders.

XIV

Fleeing the power of Trebizond was not difficult. While the armies marched out on battle-order, the donkey's Crusade trudged South through the deserted fields.

Thomas had seen the gates of Trebizond, and Brother James

88

had his own theories; it was (of course) Aubery who kept asking, 'But *why?*'

Thomas said finally, 'They are afraid of other Christians, and especially of Franks.'

'*Why?*'

'Ask Brother James.'

Perhaps even Brother James had been blinking a little, though under his thorny brows it was not easy to be sure. He said, 'Thomas told you. Years ago–but still within living memory– Frankish Crusaders treacherously attacked the Greek Christians. Not even for religious zeal: for nothing but greed. For greed of loot they took and sacked the first and most glorious city of Christendom: the city of Byzantium. What Greek will ever trust a Frank after that? And to Trebizond I think many Greeks must have fled from the sack of that city.'

Thomas put in wearily, 'The royal family of Trebizond are Comneni from Byzantium.'

'But—!' Aubery was stammering in his outrage. 'We meant them no harm! We are three unarmed men and a donkey! And they turn out an army against us! We could have explained!'

'They thought we were scouts,' Thomas said.

After a pause Brother James added quietly, 'And what could we have explained? We *are* a Frankish Crusade. We mean them no harm now, but what harm will be done to them if we are successful?'

'But Prester John isn't a Frank! Oh I see; he has offered himself as an ally of the Franks.' Aubery laughed, loudly and rudely, to make it clear that he was not suppressing tears. 'So what do we dangerous Crusaders do now, Thomas?'

'Go East,' said Brother James, before Thomas could open his mouth.

'East,' Thomas agreed.

'Well, just at the moment,' Aubery said bitterly, 'I make it that we are going almost due South. A good beginning.'

'It will get better,' said Thomas. 'Aubery, your sense of direction only works over one day. Do you think we can travel East by walking straight into the dawn? We must follow the roads.'

'Which roads?'

'There's a good road East from here. You can't see it because we're moving parallel to it, since we wouldn't be welcome on it. But we'll have to join it soon to get over the pass.'

Aubery looked at the vast glittering range barring their way at the limits of the plain, and demanded, 'What pass?'

'Aubery, can't you *see*?'

'*No*,' said Aubery violently.

Thomas had given up trying to teach either of them how to see the obvious lie of the land. To him, the very look of the range was enough to tell him that soon it would break down into ice-falls and great ravines and then the high saddle that he knew as the landmark for this road.

And so it did. Unhappily the road proved to be well used. They sat in the fringes of a pine-forest and watched it all one afternoon. Aubery said, 'If we took it quickly—' and Brother James said, 'And if we spoke to no one on the way—'

But the pass it led to was on the scale of the range it broke. The saddle at the top held a whole busy camp.

'No,' said Thomas, sighing, 'they'd know that we came from Trebizond, and Trebizond has had time to send out the alarm. We shall have to find our own way.'

They told him, of course, that it could not be done; as if anyone with eyes in his head could not see that where there was a broad pass of this kind there must be smaller ways alongside and higher. He soon grew tired of explaining and simply slapped the donkey along. He had to say for them that, once they had accepted the need, they did not grumble at the long climb, the precarious camps on sloping ledges, the blizzards that weighed them down and the icy gales that buffeted them for hours together; or even, very much, at the short rations this forced on them. What he found hard to stand was their constant mistrust of his lead. Even when he had brought them to the top, they did not believe that there could be a way down, and it was only the donkey, equally annoyed, who decided them by setting off by himself.

After a time they had the grace to apologise, and Aubery, who curiously enough had suffered from the crossing more than Brother James, added, 'I'm so turned about I don't know which way we've been making. How do you know what we'll find at the

90

bottom? Suppose it's the barbarous sea?'

'There's no sea here,' said Thomas smiling.

They rounded a shoulder and saw far below them an expanse of black water.

'A lake,' said Thomas.

They slid and jolted and trudged down to its level. The black water swirled and slapped in rustling head-high forests of reeds. Black mountains rose on both sides of it; as far as eye could see there was no farther shore.

'Thomas,' said Aubery in a small voice, 'what's the difference between a lake and the sea?'

Thomas said, 'You can drink from a lake. And you can walk all the way round it.'

Aubery burst into tears.

When they had made camp, Brother James said quietly to Thomas, 'I think the boy is ill.'

Aubery lay in his blankets shivering and dozing. Worried, Thomas asked, 'Do you know the illness?'

'Yes. Weariness. It was a hard crossing, and he is a growing boy.'

This was true; Aubery had shot up lately until he was half a head taller than Thomas, but he had had no chance to fill out; he was all knees and elbows and gaunt ribs.

'We must find somewhere to rest,' said Thomas. They had camped almost at lake level, among a grove of curiously aromatic dark trees, and while Brother James saw to the fire Thomas took Aubery's sling into the woods behind and brought down some clumsy birds with plump speckled breasts. There were tumbling streams, too, in which grew cresses he recognised as wholesome, and when he brought these back to the camp he found Brother James cooking bread-cakes on the hot stones.

'I thought we had finished the flour.'

'Whatever your hunger today, it could be greater tomorrow. I hid a bag in my bedroll.'

They fed Aubery with bread and broth made from the speckle-breasted birds; and, waking before dawn next day, Thomas climbed a few hundred feet to where he had a view of the black lake, with the clouds hanging heavy over its glooming distances.

As the sun lifted over the mountains, its rays struck through some scribbles of rising smoke.

He marked the direction, climbed down, and said to Brother James, 'Break camp. There's a village three miles on.'

'Will they welcome us?'

'We must try. Aubery needs more comfort than this dank place.'

When they came to load the donkey, he backed away; so they accepted the idea and put Aubery up, holding him on as he swayed and muttered and drowsed. Quite soon they came to a beaten path, and just before noon trotted out of the dark aromatic groves into the square of a village built on stilts above the reeds.

It was a fish village. The people caught fish, ate fish, wore fish, and smelt of fish. They were a fawn people, mild, welcoming, indecisive, and intelligent. They spoke no language known to Thomas, though he tried them with Arabic, Greek, Turkish, Persian, and some words said to be of welcome preserved so long in his family's memory that no one knew what they were. The fish-villagers were polite and patient and curious, allowing him all the time he wanted with his languages, and meanwhile examining all four of them from all sides and discussing them in low slurring tones that were not unlike the gurgle and plop of fish jumping. When Thomas gave up and resorted to the international language of signs, they entered joyfully into conversation with him, welcoming them with hands together, inviting them into huts with bows, opening their arms to make them free of everything. Aubery was guided and pushed up a ladder into a fish-smelling hut and left to be put to bed by a shoal of fawn ladies, while Thomas and Brother James and the donkey were invited to a ceremonial meal in the square.

It was the first time Thomas had ever seen the donkey defeated. In one way and another everything he was offered to eat was fish, and with one scalding look he handed the situation over to Thomas and trotted away to graze outside the village.

They had nothing to offer in exchange for this hospitality, so after supper Thomas sang for them. This pleased them highly, and they brought out some little drums made from shells with fish-skin stretched across them, very cunningly tuned, and beat them to his time and danced. They were amazingly agile at this;

really, Thomas considered, they were rather like fish, with their smooth fawn bodies and eyes glinting white.

'Of what religion are these people?' Brother James enquired.

'I haven't discovered,' Thomas admitted. 'They aren't Muslim, anyway, because they haven't prayed yet and it's long past the prayer-hour. I think, Brother James, that we should join Aubery now.' If there were to be prayers before sleep, it was prudent as well as courteous to be out of the way of them.

There were no more good-nights, when they rose, than cordial bows and waves. 'Perhaps,' Brother James suggested, 'they are like the good idolatrous people, with an idol in a temple some- where. If they expect it, Thomas, we will salute such an idol. It is the intention that matters to heaven, and our intention would be courtesy and gratitude. And tomorrow I will do what I can to cure their sick.'

This seemed both safe and satisfactory; until going out of the hut the next morning Thomas found himself in the middle of the first Muslim prayer.

He slid hurriedly to his knees and put his forehead to the ground, hoping that he had not missed too many of the prostrations.

When he had found his place, he became more than a little puzzled. He did not know the fish-villagers' language, but no Muslim prayers that he had ever heard of included an old man with a fish-mask standing up all the time; and though they were all facing the same way his sense of direction told him they were a good quarter of the compass north of Mecca: aligned, in fact, on a small hill in the plain beyond the village which seemed to have a ceremonial path leading towards it.

At the morning meal he conveyed that his companion was a healer. The fish-people were delighted with this, and a small procession of lame legs and whimpering children made its way to their hut. Thomas wanted to visit the donkey, but the old man of the fish-mask, with every appearance of bestowing a privilege, took him to see the small hill. There was something there, he conveyed, that was of special interest to him.

Cut into the top of the hill was a small amphitheatre, set with stones to make a ceremonial entrance, and in the middle of it a black and pitted stone surrounded with offerings of small and smelly dishes. The old man gave Thomas something (fishy, naturally) to make his own offering, and from the spot at which he was told to stand he could see that the stone had a resemblance to a great fish. There were lesser stones chipped and plastered with drawings, mostly of improbably large fish being struck by men with spears; but the one the old man pointed out to him was different. It was of three men with bulbous heads and new moons in their hands, and next to them was something with a double-curved line horizontal over two vertical wedges. When Thomas puzzled over that, the old man took him by the arm and pointed to the meadows where the donkey grazed.

'Horses,' said Thomas, enlightened. He pulled himself together and signalled comprehension and admiration, and the old man, delighted, gave him a piece of fish and pushed him in the direction of the donkey.

Thomas crossed the lush meadows to him.

'I've brought you this,' he said, 'but I'm afraid it's fish. They don't have anything else.'

'Thank you. Can *you* eat it?' said the donkey.

'No.' Not to be seen to be despising a gift, Thomas buried it, and sat for a time on the wonderfully grass-smelling grass and contentedly watched his donkey.

'They have good grass,' said the donkey.

'Yes, it's a nice place. But we can't stay. They were idolaters, but they were converted to Islam by cavalry with turbans and scimitars. They weren't converted very well, because they think their fish-idol is the Kaaba at Mecca, and they've got the prayers wrong; but the cavalry may come back.'

The donkey swung his heavy head towards him and remarked, 'The boy needs rest.'

'Then we must travel slowly.'

The donkey munched for some time, and then said distantly, 'Fish are caught from boats.'

Thomas gazed at him thunderstruck. And he had never thought of that himself!

They left the fish-village next day, in the boat of the old man's sons.

It was more of a punt than a boat; perhaps the fish-villagers did not venture far into the lake, or perhaps it was a ceremonial boat.

At any rate it was comfortable, with a broad deck on which Aubery could lie and drowse and a shallow well fitted out for the donkey. Four men with long poles sent it gliding through secret tunnels in the reeds, and slowly the mountains they had come over disappeared in the mists behind them, and out of the mists in front of them grew little by little the faint white lacings of snow-covered peaks.

'We go over there?' Aubery asked, a little pale. His angularities were rounding out, but he had lost his street-urchin confidence.

'No, I've been talking to the eldest son,' said Thomas. It had been teasing work in sign-language, but he had discovered that the son had travelled a little and understood how to make a map. 'This way we're going is down a long arm of the lake, and at the end of it we can join a road.'

'The Silk Road?' asked Brother James, his deep eyes giving a gleam from under the brows.

'Not yet,' said Thomas, patient with their extraordinary inability to judge distances. 'It will join the Silk Road, but farther on. Don't worry, I know now where we are.'

He meant that he had their next way clear in his mind; but also that at some point on that way—he did not know which point, but he would know when the time came—at some point soon he would see the first landmarks for the Silk Road eastwards.

XV

In these long light evenings, Brother James complained of the noisiness of the caravan. Even Aubery, who during the day enjoyed the singing and the jeering exchanges among the young folk, grew impatient with them by the time the camp-site was reached. 'One needs a little peace,' he would say austerely, jockey for a camp at the fringes of the caravan, and pitch the tent so that the door looked away into the endless desert.

They still had to suffer visits from their neighbours, with solemn exchanges of ritual compliments and tiny cups of tisane. Thomas soon found that it was mostly he who had to receive and pay these calls. If Aubery was in the rare mood for company he was off learning new songs; and as for Brother James, he would sit through the first half-hour, gaunt and impressive, and had mastered the right forms of welcome in the half-dozen different dialects in use in the caravan, but after that would rise and retire into the inner room. 'To his devotions,' Thomas would explain, and the visitors would nod with reverence and think the more of them for having such a holy man in their party. No one asked what type of devotions he professed; caravan manners prevailed. Thomas alone would sit patiently through the long hours, ensuring their welcome, picking up every tiny item of information and fitting it into his knowledge of the lands around.

It was lucky that nowadays they possessed a tent in which they could both receive visitors and make devotions. Sixteen days out from the black lake, they had got into the green twilight of a pine forest, and had appreciated there one of the gifts from the fish-villagers: a hooked hatchet that lopped branches neatly. With leather lashings they had contrived a tent-frame, which could be taken down into a bundle that rode on one of the saddle-bags. This made a square tent, with broad door-flaps opening as an outer room. Thomas had insisted on this elaboration as a mark of respectability. It called, to cover it, for more blankets than they then possessed; but a week later they fell in with a frightened party who had lost themselves in the solemn pine-masked valley, and Thomas at once offered himself as guide. The men of the party spoke something nearer to Turkish than the fish-villagers, so communication was possible on a basic level. They were not traders, but had been sent to escort the daughter of someone of importance to her wedding with someone of more importance, and now wanted to get home to somewhere with an unpro-nounceable name. Brother James and Aubery were aghast at Thomas's easy assumption that he could guide them to a place he had never heard of, and again he had to explain to them things that to him were so obvious that he could hardly put them into words.

'None of them are used to travelling, so they aren't traders, and their weapons are only for show, so they aren't soldiers, and they don't smell so they aren't fishermen; so they must be farmers. All I have to do is look out for the kind of country where farmers like that live, and when I've had a better look at their clothes and stores I'll know what kind of height they live at. As for the name, I've only heard it a couple of times, but I'll get it right before long.'

'I don't believe you can do it,' Aubery insisted.

'Well, you look round you,' Thomas said snappishly, 'and see if I'm wrong in guiding farmers who eat barley-bread out of a barren moraine.'

He sometimes wished that they understood his craft better, so that they could appreciate the way he tackled his problem. For once, religion helped him; when it came to the normally tricky time of prayers, he discovered that his clients were particularly unhappy because they revered a certain sacred mountain out of whose sight they did not like to stray. Tiringly, as well as making the usual day's march he had to scout widely. However, the chief men in the escort were elderly, and liked to rest one day in four; and on the second of these rest-days Aubery came plunging and slithering back to camp in the middle of the morning with the news that he had seen a house–could it be part of the village they were looking for?

Thomas went back with him and examined the humped little building with care from a distance.

'It's not a house,' he said at last, 'it's a summer-shepherd's hut. So somewhere down there are plains too dry to pasture flocks in summer. Oh, we're getting on very nicely. Have you got your pipe with you?'

'Yes,' said the surprised Aubery.

'Then play. I never knew a summer-shepherd who didn't like music.'

They toiled up the hill with Aubery's pipe trilling and shrilling to the blue ranges. It was tuned Western fashion, but he had become clever in adapting it to the music of these parts. Presently the summer-shepherd appeared from his hut, frantically playing his own pipe.

He was a wild figure, not easily distinguished from his own pastures, but very hospitable and delighted to hear them. He was a little mad, of course; all summer-shepherds either were or became so in the course of their work. His name seemed to be Hliakh, and he indicated the direction of his home village very

97

accurately (for Thomas) by a sideways twist of the head and a crooking of one finger. His interest was in Aubery's music and the leather flask of fermented drink their clients had given them; he hailed the look of the flask with satisfaction, and dived into his turf-roofed bothy and brought out some ferocious goat's-milk cheese to go with it. Thomas nodded to Aubery to carry on, and lay back to watch, taking in especially the cloth of Hliakh's tattered tunic and the pattern of his belt.

Hliakh's vocabulary was mostly different ways of blowing between his teeth, but Aubery got on very well with him. They exchanged tunes, and then Hliakh brought out, as a great treasure, some hollow stems not yet made up into pipes, and the two of them spent a long time making duplicates of their own pipes, which they then ceremoniously exchanged. Aubery would have stayed on, but the strain was beginning to tell on Hliakh. No one can spend eight months of the year alone but for three thousand goats, and stand the arrival of two strangers and a host of new tunes without getting madder. He began taking short runs up the slope, where he stood looking into solitude and panting, and Thomas said to Aubery, 'Time to go.'

'But you haven't asked him anything!'

'I've learnt enough.' Thomas made a business of tightening his belt and shaking out his sandals, and Hliakh embraced him with enthusiasm and plunged into his bothy to find gifts for them. To Aubery he gave some of the hollow stems, and to Thomas a very beautiful length of grass cord intricately plaited. Thomas gave him the rest of the fermented drink, and slipped Aubery a belt-length of leather for his gift. The two pipes played dementedly together for as long as they were in earshot.

'But what did you learn?' Aubery complained as he took the pipe from his lips and shook it dry.

'Where his village is. It's through that low pass to the North-east and then off South. He has the same clothes and food as our clients, but the work on his belt is different. He's of the same people but a different village . . . Aubery, most of those notes sound out of tune to me.'

Glad of the chance to be instructor in his turn, Aubery explained the Eastern modes. 'If we're going into these lands, we should be able to sing their music.'

98

'I used to, when I was a child; but then I went to the abbey and had to sing their way. You'll have to teach us, Aubery. You can have this beautiful piece of plaiting to hang your pipe on tomorrow, but tonight I need it.'

After supper he took his piece of plaiting to his clients, who seized on it with relief, and after a long discussion (quite a lot of which he understood) agreed that the people who made exactly *that* pattern lived in exactly *this* relationship to their own village.

'Three days more,' Thomas promised them, and before he left made a point of admiring their blankets, which were of thick felted goats' hair. They took the polite hint; and when, at the end of three days, they toiled over a saddle to a view of the sacred mountain and the smoke blowing from their own chimneys, Thomas was paid in magnificent blankets.

So here they were, very comfortable in the caravan. They could travel with it, Thomas reckoned, probably for another four or five weeks, depending on how long it overstayed in the towns along the road; and by that time they would be well into the Easterly lands, and it would be time for him to stretch his wits and start asking questions.

'They say we're coming to a sizeable town,' Aubery remarked, striding up beside him. At three miles an hour one could happily visit friends and gossip during the day's march.

'Good. We need stores.'

'Have we money left?'

'Plenty. And quite safe. I changed our bezants in the Baghdad caravan. I don't know what these coins are, but their weight is true.'

Now they could see the head of the caravan half a mile in front of them, because it had started up a long slope.

'The town's probably over the crest,' said Aubery with a glance at the sun. 'That town of Outremer where you found me, Thomas: was it big? I can't remember it.'

'Bigger than anything we'll find here, I think.'

'How did I live in it? This caravan's too crowded for me.'

'You're becoming a Traveller,' said Thomas in mild surprise. Travellers, in his experience, were born, not made.

Aubery laughed. 'When I was small I wanted to see all of

Outremer; when I'd seen that I wanted to see all of the world . . .
I'd like to *hear* Outremer again, though.'

'*Hear?*' Thomas listened; in the desert silence that had
surrounded them for so long, all he could hear was the jangling of
the camel bells. 'No, listen! The town is just beyond the crest.'

Very faintly came the cry of the muezzin calling. The caravan
began to halt for the hour of prayer.

'Yes, *hear!*' said Aubery vigorously. 'Not the everlasting camel
bells, not the muezzin! Just honest Christian bells in a steeple!'

They came to the top of the slope, and saw the town below, and
among its mosques rose Christian steeples, and they heard the
tolling of Christian bells calling them to Evensong.

XVI

It took all of Thomas's authority to keep them within camp that
night.

A big caravan, of course, did not go straight into a town. For
one thing there would not have been room for it, and for another
its arrival was an occasion to be celebrated. They stopped at a
camp-site outside the town limits, and presently a procession of
notables came out and presented their compliments to the master
of the caravan. That done (and it took several stately hours), a
procession of the townsfolk came out, much less impressive and
much more jolly, though here and there rather scandalous.
Seeing this, Brother James retired into their inner room. It was
more difficult to deal with Aubery, who, for all his talk of
solitude, wanted to see what was to be seen, which would probably have finished in a headache next morning. The donkey
helped Thomas with this problem by developing a limp, and
Aubery spent the first part of the evening putting compresses on
his fetlock. In the end Thomas relented so far as to take him to a
party in the neighbouring tent.

This tent was occupied by a dealer in spices who was con-
ducting the mother-in-law of his rich cousin after a long journey
that had involved two family weddings, so that the party could be

guaranteed to remain respectable. The spice-dealer recognised Thomas, and with a beseeching glance handed the respectability over to him and vanished to livelier parts. Thomas made his manners to the mother-in-law and then let himself be absorbed into a group of citizens boasting about the beauties of their town, which they called, simply, The City.

'Of course the wonders of your City are spoken of in the farthest countries I have travelled in,' he assured them politely.

Equally politely they assured him that they believed him to have travelled as far as anyone they had ever heard of, and to have spoken with all the most distinguished men there. They spoke Turkish, though with the nasal accent that seemed to grow thicker as they went Easterly. They had no curiosity about where he had been, and wanted only to boast about their City. It seemed that the family fortune was in meat, and the number and splendour of abattoirs is not an inspiring subject of conversation; but at least it gave him the chance to enquire about the geography of the town. Yes, they said, the mosque was of course in the main square, along with the government offices where they would have to go for customs examination.

'I have one donkey and two saddle-bags with our stores, worshipful citizens. My contract is to a holy man, and therefore not for profit. Will it be necessary for me to go through customs?'

Rather wordily, they decided that Thomas would not be required to pay duty but had better get the official stamp on his goods. 'The stamp of what great man?'

'Wang Khan,' they said with great assurance; which he already knew meant no more than Great Khan.

'He is of course the Khan of all this famed country?'

They agreed; he lived, they added, uncounted days towards the East, and no one here had ever had the felicity of seeing him; nor did they expect it, though someone's uncle had once had the semi-felicity of seeing his under-Khan.

Aubery, whose Turkish was coming on, said in an undertone in Frankish, 'City governor here, provincial governor farther on—whoever really rules is very much farther on yet.'

Thomas nodded to him, and pursued: 'And the number and beauty of your city buildings is famed throughout the civilised world. Tell me of them in detail.'

They did so for almost an hour, so that he could pick out what interested him. 'A temple? What kind of a temple?'

They said carelessly, 'Of some curious religious sect; you can't expect good Muslims to keep all their names in mind.'

'A temple of another religion in a Muslim town?' Thomas was a little shocked. 'That is surely contrary to the Law of the Prophet.'

They were even more shocked at the suggestion. Of course they never went near the abominable places, nor had ever looked at the idolatrous pictures displayed upon them, though they had to admit that to truly cultured people their effect was not disagreeable.

'I admit correction,' Thomas said penitently. 'It is only that in other lands that I have known heathen temples were not permitted.'

'We can see that you are a man of great experience,' they said generously. 'But, as you say, our glorious land is new to you, and we have other customs. Our Great Khan, on whom be the blessing, has ordered things differently here. Here, our Great Khan has unequivocally stated, those who wish to be damned are allowed to be damned, and no one has the right to stop them.'

'It is a view showing great breadth of vision,' Thomas said cautiously. 'If it is permissible to ask—the Great Khan himself—?'

It was quite possible, they allowed, that the Great Khan himself was among the damned. He lived in the farthest East, which as everyone knew was the resort of a great many kinds of devil, and very little was known about him personally. But he had commanded that everyone should be allowed to worship in his own way, and those who had never tried it would be surprised to find how peaceful this method of rule made the land.

'Religious tolerance?' Aubery said doubtfully; and they said certainly not: very numerous cavalry.

'Our holy man,' said Thomas, 'who like all holy men is curious in such matters, will find this of absorbing interest. Please tell us more. For example, I saw a building of unfamiliar shape, a pointed tower that rang bells. What type of damnation resides there?'

Whoever were the Christians in this town, he noted, they were not many, because his informants had to consult together before they could be sure. 'Oh yes, in that alley behind the square. I don't know what they call themselves; they're very poor and some kind of refugee. Their sign is a cross.'

'Exiled heretics,' Aubery said as they made their way back to their own tent.

'I'm afraid so. But this Great Khan—what do you think of him?'

'He's a long way away.'

'Yes,' Thomas agreed, sighing, 'so we must go through his lands to come to Prester John. Well, his religious policy will make for easy travelling: that's something to be grateful for . . . It's a funny policy, isn't it? Do you want to visit these Christians?'

'Not very much,' Aubery said frankly, 'but Brother James will insist.'

He was right; Brother James at once had one of his attacks of responsibility for Aubery's spiritual welfare, and insisted that he should go the next morning to hear Mass; but characteristically added, 'And no doubt some good Christians will then greet us, and may be able to give us information not known to your friends tonight. And Thomas, though I would not wish to deprive you of the comforts of religion, it does appear to me that you might get better information if it were seen that you had not been to the Christian church.'

The next morning they started with the customs officials in the main square. Thomas was impressed by their efficiency. When he asked advice about changing one of his gold coins, the officer promptly weighed it and gave him half the weight in silver and half in some tokens current in the town, and took only one token commission. They looked at the mosque, which was medium-provincial only, but they loudly admired it. Then they parted, arranging to meet in the market three hours after noon.

Thomas had a very good day. The local methods of baking were new to him, and he went from stall to stall, enquiring and tasting and dickering, before he bought a quantity of hard-baked biscuit packed in a kind of leaf, some wind-dried meat in strips, and a few packs of a dried fruit that was full of seeds but very sweet and guaranteed sustaining. He also renewed his little bag of salt and his store of leather and thread, and, after counting his tokens, was able to replenish Brother James's stock of medicines. Finally he went back to the main square, hitched the donkey to a rail outside the liveliest of the inns, kicked off his shoes, and ordered his mid-day meal.

Here Brother James and Aubery found him, and had difficulty in detaching him from an acquaintance who years before had travelled with a man who had travelled with three grandsons of Uncle Joseph. Thomas was feeling pleased with the world and with himself. Solitary though Travellers may be, none is entirely happy unless he can pick up his people's fine-spun lines of communication.

Brother James and Aubery were less happy. They walked back to the camp together, and Brother James gave courteous attention to Thomas's doings, but did not speak of their own until Thomas thought to ask.

'Well: we have been to Mass; but I am not clear in my mind that we were welcome.'

Aubery said scornfully, 'A wretched lot they are: afraid to open their mouths.'

'What have they got to be afraid of?'

'As heretics and exiles,' said Brother James, excusing them, 'they have been persecuted for generations. It seems that they are hardly capable now of believing that they are not in danger.'

'Had they ever heard of Prester John?'

'I did not judge it useful to ask.'

It seemed to Thomas, on the way back to the camp, that the donkey hung forward on his halter, as if he thought they should hurry. Aubery came to help him unpack his stores, and instead of admiring his bargains said abruptly, 'When does the caravan leave?'

'In about a week, I should think. There are new people coming, and stores to be bought . . . Is something the matter?'

For the boy—but he was too tall now to be called a boy—was fidgeting, but not idly; instead of stacking the new stores, he was putting them into the saddle-bags. 'Matter? I'm not sure. I met a girl—'

'A girl?' Thomas stopped thunderstruck. It had never occurred to him before that Aubery was of an age now to meet a girl and not forget her. He got into a flurry, wondering what to do about it. There had he been, noticing how tall the boy was, and quite ignoring that he was well set up with it, and in these parts noticeable with his yellow Frankish hair: just the kind of boy a girl might cast a kindly eye at. He began, 'I can do this unpacking alone, if you want to—'

Aubery gave a shout of laughter. 'Thomas, don't be a fool!'

'I beg your pardon, Aubery.'

'She wanted my advice about getting married. She wanted to know if we had travelled anywhere where a Christian could marry a Muslim in peace.'

'Well–can't they here?'

'No. She's Christian and wants to marry this Muslim camel-driver, and neither his family nor hers will hear of it.'

'What did you tell her?'

'No,' said Aubery bleakly; and then stopped, because the donkey was moving.

This was startling enough, because he had not yet had his supper; but there was so much decision in the way he lifted his head, twitched his ears, and trotted off south that they followed him without a word.

Since Aubery had chosen their camp-site, at ten paces to the south of it they were in the desert. When the donkey halted, the camp-fires were too distant to illumine them, but he put his head down and looked unwaveringly into the darkness. After a moment something fluttered white and a voice breathed, 'Is it Aubery?'

'Rachel? What are you doing here?'

'You said you were camped this side. Wait, I've a lantern; stand close.' Under the shadow of their cloaks a yellow glow blossomed and showed a girl with a veil over her dark head. With relief Thomas saw that she was no beauty whom Aubery could moon after, but a plump young woman with a round cheerful face now puckered in distress. 'You silly boy, you didn't do as I said!'

'This is Thomas.'

'Good Traveller, will *you* listen to advice?'

'I think,' Thomas said soberly, 'that Aubery did listen, Mistress Rachel. Did you warn him to leave?'

'You're so *slow*,' Rachel complained. 'That was hours ago.'

'Rachel, we're with the caravan; and we hadn't bought our stores; and you only said you suspected—'

'Well, it's more than suspicion now. I've heard them talking, my father and the other elders. You're so stupid, how did you ever imagine they'd welcome you?'

Thomas said, 'We were told that there is religious toleration in the town.'

'Oh I daresay!' she snapped scornfully; 'I daresay you were *told*! And I daresay you imagined that not being allowed to massacre one another makes them love one another.'

'I thought you wanted to marry a Muslim, mistress.'

Rachel began to cry. 'Of course I do. It's all so *stupid*. Perhaps it's not the religion after all, perhaps it's just because they're not prosperous and not respected and they think they'll be praised if they unmask a band of Western spies.'

'*Spies*?' said Thomas and Aubery together; even the donkey swung his head to look at her mildly.

'Well, what else can they denounce you for, if it isn't a crime to be Christians?'

'But whose spies?'

'Oh how should I know? Any of those Westerners the Great Khan is going to conquer as soon as he has time. I tell you I've heard them talking. Are you quite mad to be still hanging about here?'

XVII

'So you want to travel to the court of the Great Khan,' the master of the caravan said to Thomas.

Deferentially—for it was an honour to be received in the master's tent—and trying to conceal his nervousness—for he had walked nine miles around to conceal the fact that the donkey, with Brother James and Aubery and their baggage, had quietly left the caravan four hours ago—Thomas said, 'My client is a holy man.'

'Well, we know holy men,' said the master, eating candied fruit.

'They must go,' said Thomas, quoting a Travellers' proverb, 'always a little farther.'

In appreciation the master gave him some fruit. 'And of course they never realise how far that is going to be. I will say this for them, though: they don't grumble. Ask questions for ever, perhaps, but grumble, no.'

'I will answer for my holy man there.'

'But what was your contract?' said the master, coming to the crux of the problem.

'Indefinite.'

'Where there is land,' said the master, pouring himself a drink, 'there must be roads, and where there are roads the Traveller can go, if he knows the water-holes and the landmarks.' He put the water-holes first, showing that he was a man of the deserts. 'But round here few choose to go far these days. We keep up the trading-routes, that's all.'

'Yet they tell me that the lands are at peace, and well policed.'

'Oh, they are. The Great Khan, on whom be the blessing, insists on that: proper policing, prompt payment of tribute–the two go together, as an experienced man like yourself must have noticed. It takes the interest out of travelling, in my view. I am a short-haul man and not ashamed of it. I make a good living, and at home I have twenty-seven children to keep an eye on, and you can't do that if you take the long hauls.'

Thomas expressed suitable admiration of the number of his children and the quality of his care for them (which was indeed unusual in his trade); then added slyly, 'But in the years before you became a family man, excellency?'

The master shifted in embarrassment, and pushed over to Thomas a cup of his drink, which was a very brisk cordial; he kept his countenance as a Muslim by having it slightly warmed. 'It is undeniable that as a young man I was ambitious to make great journeys. It was said not to be possible, because we had the misfort— had the pleasure of being on the line of march of the Great Khan's armies. As armies go, they were well behaved; I am not a poor man, to begrudge a camel or two or a few sacks of grain in taxes, and once the officials were at their posts the demands were clearly set out, so that one could adjust one's accounts for a favourable assessment. But one did prefer to meet the armies—if I make myself clear—standing among trusty friends whose interests were similar.'

'That is wholly understandable. This was when the Great Khan's armies were moving West to attack the Muslims there?'

'Both East and West. The Great Khan moves with such speed that we had hardly got the warehouses straight after his going than they had to be turned upside down again for his return.'

'Return?' said Thomas warily. 'Were his armies defeated in the West?'

'Certainly not,' said the master, scandalised. 'The Great Khan is totally undefeatable. His armies are as the sands of the sea, and as you know there can be no greater number than that, and move at such speed because each rider has ten horses with him. No, he died, away Easterly in his homelands, so his armies had to return for the election of his successor.'

'Ah. When you speak of the Great Khan you refer to whoever holds the title at the time?'

'Naturally. As to who he is personally, that hardly concerns us.'

'True. But we were speaking of the past, excellency.'

'We were.' The master poured them both more of the cordial. 'When the coming of the armies was only a rumour. Yes, I was barely twenty, but I remember those days; one went a couple of days East and somehow knew that something was coming; the desert was so silent . . . But East I would go, swearing to make a great journey. Ah, good days!' He drank to them.

'It was plain to me at once that you were a man by nature bold; though also, as the master of a caravan, properly prudent. Did you meet the armies in those good days?'

'No. Well, I was distracted from my purpose. It was a good journey nonetheless, and a record in my family. I can tell you the landmarks, though you must understand that it is the political situation that counts now.'

'Your Excellency's generosity passes even its reputation among wise men. Little though my gifts are worthy of your acceptance—'

Thomas began to lay them out, but was unexpectedly waved

back. 'It does my heart good to see a true Traveller again,' the master said sentimentally. 'Just such a one was I, once.' He consented to accept a belt of plaited thongs, a pattern Thomas had adapted from the summer-shepherd Hliakh, and told him the landmarks, ending beatifically (for he had to have several cups of cordial to sharpen his memory), 'And may you too be distracted from your purpose and settle down as a short-haul man.'

'Sir?' said Thomas, startled.

'I brought back my chief wife from that trip. A Kerait she was, though not so attached to her own people that she hasn't been a good Muslim all these years, and looked after the business most capably while I was away.'

'The Keraits must be an estimable people. Of course you have escorted your wife on her visits to her parents.'

'In fact, no. In fact, her parents were under the impression that she was marrying another man altogether. Luckily I possessed in those days a *mehari* of remarkable speed. I will show you him,' said the master, wiping a happy tear; 'we kept him as a souvenir of our wedding.'

He was a rug, worn almost hairless. Hopefully, Thomas asked, 'And are the Keraits East of the Great Khan?'

'East? . . . by no means. Young Traveller, we are speaking of far-travelling, but as far-travels exceed short-hauls, so do the domains of the Great Khan exceed far-travelling. Look now!' He pulled himself up on his elbow to find a charred stick in the ashes below the brazier, and drew a plan with it. 'As I understand it—you realise that I am not speaking from experience: here is The City. Over there by your foot—' Thomas was sitting cross-legged on his left— 'are the lands in the West that the Great Khan was in the process of conquering when he died and had to be re-elected: Harimin I have heard them called. Here—' He slapped down his right hand— 'is the land of the Keraits. And just so far away again, they say, are the homelands of the Great Khan.'

Thomas felt his heart sink. 'Are his people the farthest East of any peoples?'

'Oh, I think so. If their numbers are as the sands of the sea, with ten times as many horses, how would there be room for any other peoples?'

'And their religion?'

'Who knows? They say not Muslim, because he conquers without converting. In my view, that fails to allow for the speed of his advance, which doesn't leave time for the usual method of dealing with the heathen.' He drew his finger across his throat. 'Quite possibly he will deal with conversions after conquests. But in Asia there are countless other religions he might favour. His wife, for example, is of some curious unknown religion–a fact I know because she is a Kerait, like my chief wife. There are even a few of them in The City, though not of the social class I would want my chief wife to mix with.'

'What would they be called?' Thomas asked faintly.

'We don't mix, I tell you. All I know of them is that they say the wrong prayers at the wrong time and worship a cross.'

Thomas slipped discreetly away from the caravan towards the South, made a long weary circuit, and presently heard a hiccuping snort ahead of him, and in the starlight saw shining the long white nose of his donkey.

'I hoped you'd be waiting for me, Ears. Take me to the camp, please.'

The donkey swung round and trotted off, and after a mile or so stopped on a fold in the stony floor where no camp could possibly be; only a good smell and the faintest glow of a hidden fire marked where Aubery was cautiously cooking.

'We thought we had best not be seen,' he said. Brother James drew aside the screen to the inner room and gave Thomas a long drink.

Thomas kicked off his sandals and ducked into the tent. 'Ouf! That was a long walk. You've found a good camp.'

'Are they searching for us?' Aubery asked. At first he had been jubilant to have saved them from a threat, but now he was sulky and resentful in reaction.

'Not from the caravan; but best to be cautious. Come in, Aubery; I've news.'

Aubery brought in their meal; they sat cross-legged around the bowl, and when they had satisfied the worst of their hunger Brother James said, 'And now tell us.'

Between mouthfuls Thomas told them what he had heard from

the caravan master; then he cleaned his bowl with the last piece of bread and leant back in comfort. 'Now–you see what this means? Remember the Baghdad caravan, and how men thought there was something threatening in the East? Remember the Khwarismians, who were invading the lands of the emirs, and then disappeared?'

'That–the something threatening in the East–was this Great Khan?' Aubery guessed.

'Yes; or rather not this one, but his predecessor. He destroyed the Khwarismians, and would have turned against the emirs if he hadn't died.'

'That name,' Brother James said: 'what was it?'

'Harimin: yes, Khwarism.'

'But we saw no wars.'

'Have you forgotten? We turned North after the donkey was stolen. And then the Great Khan died, and his armies withdrew, back to their homelands in the far East.'

Aubery drew a long breath. 'When the donkey was stolen– Thomas, do you remember that I said then, why did he let himself be taken so far North by the thieves? Could he have known about the coming of the Great Khan?'

It was a tempting thought; but his donkey, Thomas felt strongly, was possessed of no such supernatural powers; his donkey was merely intelligent and experienced. 'I don't think he knew; it's very likely that he thought it wise to keep out of the way.'

Brother James was staring at them under his thorny brows. 'The Great Khan,' he said abstractedly. 'Thomas, what did you say they called him in the local language?'

'What? Oh–Wang Khan.'

Brother James repeated it in a curious thin voice. 'Wang Khan. Ouang Khan. Ohan Khan . . . And you say that he had a Christian wife?'

'Johan. John,' said Aubery in a shaking voice.

In the silence that followed, the door of the tent bulged, and the long pale nose of the donkey appeared in the gap.

Aubery put out an unsteady hand to pat it. 'Here's the whole Crusade assembled,' he said, trying to keep his voice steady. 'Brother Donkey, what is your view? Can the Great Khan be our

III

Prester John?'

The donkey swung his head so that his deep-lidded eyes fixed on Thomas.

There was a very long pause.

Then Thomas bowed his head; and the donkey backed out and let the door drop to behind him.

'Brothers,' said Thomas, 'there is only one way to find out. We must seek out the Great Khan himself.'

XVIII

'And that desert,' they had said at the last village, 'you had better pass as quickly as possible, because there are devils in it.'

'What do they look like?' Thomas had asked.

'You don't see them, you hear them. They use human voices to call for help, and so to lure you to your death in the waterless desert.'

'I see. Is there a powerful spell against them?'

'A very powerful one: take no notice. They are incorporeal and can do no other harm.'

'And you can't tell us any more about the court of the Great Khan?'

'Khans of all kinds,' they had said decidedly, 'we leave alone. In that way we hope to induce them to leave us alone.'

'Do they?' Aubery asked with interest.

'No. The tribute demanded is heavy. But they could leave us alone less. The village hasn't been sacked lately.'

That had been eight dusty days ago, and they had been travelling distressfully slowly and were still some way short of the next water. This was entirely due to Brother James, who had begun by seeing good camp-sites much too early in the day and gone on to walking with a heavy limp which he denied the moment he was asked about it. Now, with the sun sinking behind the dead desert at their backs and a bare cupful left in the last water-skin, his leg had given way and he sat on the dry grey ground with an expression of deep distaste on his face.

'An old injury,' he said distantly, and let Thomas look at his knee, which was hot and swollen.

Aubery unstrapped the food-bag and water-skin from the donkey. 'Tell me again the landmarks for the water-hole.'

'You'll have the sun at your back for the next half-hour. Keep it barely on your left shoulder, and look out for two rocks set like two fists on your right hand. They say there are trees there, so that may be the better mark.'

Aubery pulled his head-cloth over his nose and mouth, took a careful sighting on the setting sun, and with a nod looped the donkey's halter over his arm and trudged off.

It occurred to Thomas, as he watched them go, that once (how long ago?–too long to remember) he could not have allowed Aubery to go off on his own; in fact, that Aubery would have quailed at the idea. And as he thought this a disturbing thing happened: a thing which had not happened since the borders of Trebizond. Departing, the donkey turned to look at Thomas, and laying back his ears and stretching out his head to him said, *'Take care! Take care! Take care!'*

'And what,' said Brother James severely when the two shapes had blurred and faded into the lavender haze ahead: 'what was that about?'

'I don't know,' Thomas said uneasily. He looked around him. The desert looked exactly as it had looked for the last eight days, a circle of lavender-brown haze broken only by the lumpish shapes of shallow dunes, with spidery wisps of dead and barren thorn and a faint furring of brown grass grown glassy in the sun. Even if Aubery were delayed, they had water and food; the nights grew icy with the sinking of the sun, but they had blankets and he could find fuel; in this desolation there were no harmful animals. Scooping out a comfortable couch in the sand, he said, 'They warned us about devils, you remember, but all their harm is in words. Have your blankets, brother, and I'll get firing.'

'Words,' said Brother James broodingly, huddling the blankets over his gaunt shoulders. 'To devils one should not listen . . . Or perhaps one should give them religious instruction.'

Thomas shot him a look, wondering if he might be feverish. 'Can you kindle this armful while I fetch more?'

Brother James took the flint and steel, and Thomas padded off towards a long shadow that looked as if it might be bushes. The dry stuff burnt well, but too quickly; he must gather a sizeable pile. Perhaps the donkey had been warning him that Brother James was more ill than he would admit?

That was a possibility to be kept in mind; a feverish man could take harm in the desert chill. He found a parched stem and tugged at it; the roots were iron-hard and lasted well in a fire. It came out whole, spilling him backwards, and he picked himself up, stacked it, and looked around. Would there be more roots on the other side of this slope?

'Try a bit to the south.'

That took him out of sight of the tiny orange glow of the fire, but there was a whole dead grove here. He worked for a time, tearing up the wood and cracking it under his heel into good lengths, and then took fright that he had been away too long. Would the fire be out? He hoisted a faggot to his shoulder and started off.

'Not that way.'

Of course it was this way. You couldn't deceive a Traveller.

But who had spoken?

Twice. And he had not noticed.

He went at a trot back to the fire. Brother James seemed to be muttering to himself, and though there was still brushwood at his side he had let the fire dangerously low. Thomas knelt and built it up.

'Brother James, please be careful with the fire. It will be very cold soon. I'll stack the faggots where you can reach them. And Brother James, I think there's a devil over there.'

'Very likely,' said Brother James. 'There is one hereabouts. Is it trying to snatch your soul?'

'I don't think so. It was trying to make me lost.'

'Did it tempt you to mortal sin?'

It was difficult to think of a mortal sin possible just here. Then Thomas remembered that he had almost let the fire out, and said firmly, 'Yes.'

'Then defy it!' said Brother James with a shout. When Thomas had gone ten steps he called him back. 'No, Thomas, I mistake. Do not defy it. Give it religious instruction.'

'Yes, Brother James,' said Thomas, and trailed back to his wood-gathering. Brother James was certainly worse than he had thought, but what shook his confidence was the devil. Twice it had spoken to him, and he had not even been startled. It seemed wise to keep away from the spot where he had first heard it. He got a good armful of faggots together before anything else happened. Then someone near called sharply, 'Help me!' and then, farther and faintingly, 'Oh help, oh help me!' He started to run, calling, 'Aubery! Where?'; and came to himself with his faggots scattered over ten yards behind him and the dawning of a very bad temper. This must be devilry. He had known he could not expect Aubery for hours, and the voice had not even been Aubery's, and yet he had started to run like any fool. He was not any fool; he was an experienced Traveller, and resented having tricks played on him. He deliberately turned his back on the voice and gathered his wood.

It called again, from in front of him.

He snapped, 'Oh be quiet!'

The voice trailed off in the middle of a word. After a moment it said brightly, from a different spot, 'Good water over here!'

'Nonsense.'

It imitated, rather badly, a trotting horse, but as Thomas once again turned his back made a rude noise and fell silent.

Another voice, loud and close to Thomas's elbow, said admiringly, 'That's the way to deal with him!'

'And you be quiet too.'

'Not *me*,' the voice said; 'I'm your friend. I told you where to find the firewood.'

'Yes, and the wrong way back.'

'You didn't have to go back.'

'You're not my friend. You're a devil, trying to snatch my soul.'

'Can I snatch your soul?' said the voice. 'Would I like it? What is a soul?'

Thomas puzzled over this. 'If you're a devil you ought to know what a soul is. Aren't you a devil?'

'I don't think so,' said the voice. 'What is a devil? I am an incorporeal spirit.'

'So is a devil; I think. Are you from hell?'

'No,' said the voice with more confidence. 'I'm not from anywhere. I am always here in this desert. Where is hell?'

'Then why did you try to entice me into the desert?'

'For some conversation.'

'*Help me, oh help me?*' said Thomas warmly: 'do you call that conversation?'

'That wasn't me. That was one of the others. They have no imagination. Because *Help me* has worked once or twice they never think of anything else.'

'And they lead travellers away from the path.'

'But all we want,' said the incorporeal spirit, 'is a little conversation. It's very dull in this desert. Nothing happens but travellers going through it. We would like to hear news and opinions. But what happens? We invite you to talk to us, and first you refuse and then you lie down and sulk for ever.'

'Lie down and—? We *die*. Die from lack of water.'

'Water I know, I think; it runs away? What is *die?*' asked the spirit.

Thomas sat down and thought. It was getting very cold, which did not help thinking. 'There have been misapprehensions,' he said at last. 'I shall be very pleased to talk to you, but first I have to collect firewood. Will you stop interrupting until I have enough?'

'And then you'll come back and talk?'

'I promise. Oh, and another thing.'

'Yes?'

'Stop your friends talking to my companion over there. He's not well.'

'Him?' said the spirit: 'no one's talking to him. He's doing it all himself.'

When Thomas returned to Brother James, he found him, though with a curious air of having more important things on his mind, quite brisk and keeping the fire well up. Thomas heated half their water to make him a tisane, and as he worked said casually, 'I think they may not be devils after all.'

Brother James said composedly, 'I had come to that conclusion myself.'

'Oh? So I thought, if you don't mind being left, I'll go and talk to them. I might hear something of interest.'

'If you are tired, there is no need. I have the matter well in hand myself,' said Brother James statelily. 'But if you wish go by all means.'

Thomas wrapped his own blanket round his shoulders and toiled back into the desert. 'You'll have to come here,' he said to the air in front of him, not knowing how to find the incorporeal spirit, 'because I have to keep an eye on the fire.'

The incorporeal voice said at once, 'That bright stuff? That's another of the things your people love so much. What is its attraction?'

'It keeps us alive.' There was a baffled silence, and, sighing, Thomas added, 'I can't explain these corporeal things to you. We need warmth and water, that's all.'

'You are very complex.'

'You could surely have understood that.'

'You could surely have told us,' the voice retorted.

The cold was numbing Thomas's ears and lips, and he was very tired. He mumbled, 'There were faults on both sides. Can we arrange things better?'

'Will you tell us things? Why do you people appear at one edge of this desert and disappear at the other? It has always puzzled us.'

'We come from one place and go to the next.'

The spirit said wistfully, 'There are other places, then? We've never been quite sure. And one place differs from another?'

'Of course.'

'Not in this desert. Every part of this desert is the same as every other part. What rich lives you must lead!'

'There are dangers in it,' Thomas said consolingly.

'Dangers as well! You are indeed lucky. And when,' said the spirit, reverting to its grievance, 'all we can share of this richness is the knowledge of it, even that you keep to yourselves!'

'It was a misunderstanding,' Thomas said sadly. 'And after so long it will be difficult to set it right. But you can try. Listen. What my people need is water, fuel, and the right road. If you want them to be friendly, you must help them to find these things. Let me explain how to do that.'

As incorporeal spirits went, it was very intelligent. It was also very willing to try, though he suspected that what really attracted it was the possibility of a change of occupation. And, as he had hoped, it proved pressingly grateful.

'This is going to revolutionise our lives. What can we do for you in return?'

Thomas pulled his blanket closer and tucked his numbed fingers under his elbows.

'Two things, please. First of all, speak sharply to me if you see my eyes close. And secondly, tell me everything you have ever heard about the lands to the East of this desert.'

When Aubery and the donkey, with a full water-skin, found Brother James, he was still in his burrow of sand, raking together the embers and talking with confidence of having the situation well in hand. He did not know where Thomas was, and, disquietingly, had not attempted to find him. The donkey for once hurried himself, swinging this way and that, twitching his ears back and forth, before he set off into the darkness at his rare canter.

'Take no notice of devils,' said Brother James, as Aubery disappeared at the end of the halter. 'I have that under my consideration.'

There was no time to think about voices, for Thomas was not a mile away, burrowed half into the ground and too frozen to give more than a croak in answer to Aubery's anxious questions. It took a good deal of hauling and rubbing to get him to his feet and back to the fire, and Aubery was the more worried because his remarks did not always seem sensible. The donkey stood at his back while Aubery fed the fire to a blaze and made hot tisane for them both. Thomas nodded and wheezed in gratitude, but Brother James simply did as he was told.

'On to camp,' said Aubery at last in desperation. 'Come on, Brother Donkey, we've got to get them there somehow.'

Brother James, nodding, said, 'That will be included in my review of the situation,' and allowed himself to be heaved on to the donkey. Aubery went on his right to prop him up. Thomas said to the air, 'Goodbye and good luck,' and went on his left, stumbling along with one arm round the donkey's strong neck. The donkey's great ears twitched, and Aubery said, 'Did I hear something?'

'No need to worry now,' said Thomas. Even in his hurry Aubery had taken care to mark the path with cairns of kicked-up sand, and within the hour they saw the loom of the few poor trees that managed to survive around the water-hole. Aubery had not only pitched the tent before he left, but lit a fire and found a man at a neighbouring tent–there was a small caravan going West, a wretchedly poor one–who had agreed to keep it going.

'They both look in a bad way to me,' said this man, piling the fire while Aubery got Brother James and Thomas into the shelter of the tent and pulled blankets around them. 'Was it the voices led them astray?'

'What voices?' said Aubery.

'No,' said Thomas from inside the tent.

The man, who said his name was Tukhanamu (or something similar), in spite of his poverty had put his own cooking-pot on the fire with some barley porridge in it, and fed it to Thomas, who began to recover. Brother James merely motioned him away. To Aubery, who was biting his lip in dismay, Tukhanamu said, 'Boil some water in your pot, I have something for him,' and went off into his own tent. Thomas emerged from his blanket and said plaintively, 'I could eat something more solid than this.'

Aubery added some dried meat to the porridge, and Tukhanamu came back with a small bag of oiled silk, saying, 'Is the water boiling? It must be really boiling.' He threw something dark into Brother James's cup, nursed it until the water was clear and amber-coloured, and took it into the tent.

'He won't take anything,' Aubery said anxiously.

Tukhanamu came out with the cup empty. 'Asleep,' he reported.

'Share our meal,' said Aubery, who seemed to have taken command tonight.

'Oh, I've eaten. Just a mouthful, then, to keep you company,' said Tukhanamu. 'Well, you eat well, I must say. Plenty of stores?'

'Enough for guests,' said Aubery, filling his bowl again.

Tukhanamu confessed, 'We're on half-rations.' They urged him politely on until he had finished the pot and lay back with a happy sigh.

Aubery said correctly, 'Your herb has given our companion a good night's sleep, and you will allow us to repay the debt with some of our stores. But what possessed you to come out so poorly stocked?'

Tukhanamu, very relaxed and sleepy, started a long and complex story about some official who had been persecuting his family on account of an old quarrel about fences. They had to keep pulling him up because he would stray from the kitchen-Turkish they were using into some strange language.

'I'm sorry,' he said apologetically. 'This language you spoke to me in, I can get on in it well enough for a time, because we're tent-makers in my family and have to deal with the passing trade. But it's not my own language.'

Thomas said, 'What is your language? Is it Mongol?'

'We are Mongols.'

'Can you teach me some of it?'

'With pleasure.'

It was hard for Thomas to keep awake, but before Tukhanamu left he had taught him the Mongol for the Travellers' basic vocabulary; which is, roughly, *Good day, goodbye, yes, no, how much? too much, please, thank you*, and *your land/people/great ruler/products are justly famed throughout all civilised lands*. He was a squat man, even though starved-looking, with black hair, pale skin, and narrow dark eyes. He looked with disbelief at Aubery's yellow and Thomas's sandy hair. 'Is it part of your religion to paint it?' he asked. On going he asked permission to examine some technical point about the frame of their tent, and finished by saying, 'I don't like the look of your friend there.' Brother James, though peacefully sleeping, had a gaunt sunken look about his face.

Aubery burst out, when he had gone, 'How did you know he was a Mongol? That's not a name I've ever heard.'

Thomas slid limply to his knees and burrowed for his blankets. 'I heard it for the first time tonight. I'll explain when I wake up.'

XIX

Next morning none of them woke until Tukhanamu came tapping on the tent-poles.

'I don't want to disturb you, but I couldn't leave without saying goodbye and thank you for the stores.'

'Thank you,' Aubery muttered drowsily, 'for your welcome company—and information—and for keeping up our fire last night—'

'And a gift on parting,' said Tukhanamu, and pressed on them a bag of oiled silk containing something that looked rather grubby. 'It made your friend sleep last night. A herb from the East, for most ills including general debility and travellers' fatigue. Infuse in boiling water and drink as hot as possible.'

They waved his starveling little caravan into the lavender-brown haze, and hurriedly fed the donkey, who was giving them a hard stare to point out that this water-hole grew nothing he could reach but spiny thorn. Aubery said, 'He did drink the Eastern herb, but shouldn't he have feverfew?'

They looked at the Eastern herb. It was black: some kind of sun-dried leaf that emitted a pleasantly astringent smell. 'Shall we try it ourselves?' said Thomas. 'Last night's cold is still in my bones.'

They had no specific ills to cure, but the amber liquid made them feel cured. 'We'll give it to Brother James as well as feverfew,' Aubery decided. 'Did Tukhanamu say what it was called?'

He had not; so they called it Eastern tisane. When they had succeeded in awakening Brother James, he consented to take a little of the feverfew, but the Eastern tisane he drank like the rarest of wines. They went on making it for him during the day, and the only sign of recognition he gave was when he saw it approaching him. Otherwise he lay still and watched the tent-roof with every appearance of holding intelligent conversation with it. Thomas looked at his knee; the swelling was less.

They sat down at last, the sun well up and burning away the

mists, to a cross between breakfast and the midday meal.

'I think,' said Aubery, 'that his knee is nothing but an excuse. You know how stubborn he is. I think it's a case of travellers' fatigue.'

'You had it once,' Thomas recalled.

'Never . . . Oh–that time we were on a boat and you kept telling me about things that had happened that I hadn't noticed. Well, I was young then. Now: you were saying some very odd things last night. Explain, please.'

Chewing, the donkey moved up behind Thomas's shoulder.

'Did Tukhanamu give us plenty of that Eastern tisane?'

'It goes on getting darker,' Aubery said, looking at the dregs in his cup. 'Suppose we made it in the bowl and went on adding hot water?'

They discovered that one pinch in the bowl gave them cup after cup of the aromatic brew. 'This will last us for weeks,' said Aubery, looking into the bag. 'And if it comes from the East we'll be able to get more—'

Thomas said gently, 'We had best make it last.'

The donkey's nose touched his shoulder.

Aubery put down the bag with a sigh. 'Did you have dreams in the desert?'

'You didn't hear voices on your way?'

'Well–once I thought I heard you, calling me back. But the donkey made me go on. And later, when you said goodbye, I thought I heard an echo.'

Thomas told him about the incorporeal spirit; which made him envious. 'I wish I'd heard it. And it could tell you news?'

'In a way. It repeated what it had heard in the desert over the years.' A shiver ran down Thomas's backbone, and he reached for the bowl and refilled his cup. 'Oh Aubery, it was so cold! I thought I should have died of the cold. And it had heard men dying of the cold, and dying of thirst, and dying of fear of the desert. And it didn't understand any of it; it repeated it all to me . . . But other things too.'

'Prester John,' said Aubery. Under his deep weather-tan he could not grow pale, but his tight lips lost their colour.

'Yes. It wasn't even difficult to make out. Aubery, there was never any Prester John.'

'Well,' said Aubery. Looking around him, he spied a buckle that was working loose of its strap, and taking it up began to unravel it. 'It was the old story, I suppose?' he said. 'They wanted him to exist so badly that they made him up out of a couple of old legends and a few mistakes?'

'The great kingdom in the East is the kingdom of the Mongols. The first Great Khan of the Mongols, the one who conquered almost as far as Outremer, was called Jenghiz (that means Strong). He's dead; while he lived, they say he conquered from the lands of dawn to the lands of night, and now his domains stretch so far that no one man can rule them all. The Great Khan today is a grandson, Mongka, and under him the farthest East is ruled by Kubilai, and the West by Hulagu. And they say that Hulagu is leading his armies West again.'

'And of course they wouldn't be Christian.'

'No. Though we did hear rightly that there was a Christian Queen. But that doesn't mean anything, it seems. The Mongols don't care for religion. Their only religion, they say, is to conquer from one horizon to the other.'

Aubery slanted his head to one side and with great care cut away the worn threads. 'And this famous letter to the Pope?'

Thomas found him fresh thread to finish the repair. 'It seems that it's the custom for the Great Khan to write to the rulers of the lands he means to invade. He offers them, if they submit at once, peace and religious freedom under his rule; if they don't submit, he promises to destroy them. And keeps that promise. He would write in the Mongol language, of course, and at some point the letter must have been translated. Perhaps the translator misunderstood; perhaps he was afraid to write down such a threat to the Holy Father; perhaps he was mischievous. It doesn't really matter now, does it?'

'Not the smallest bit,' said Aubery, and stabbed the leather to make holes for his thread. 'Whence—' He thrust a thread through with each savage word— 'the Donkey's Crusade? From Outremer to the ends of Asia, all for the sake of nothing. Four fools on a useless journey.'

Four fools! Horrified, Thomas turned to look at the donkey, expecting to see him lining Aubery up for a double slap of his hind hooves. But at his side the long white nose and deep-lidded eyes of his donkey looked mildly at them.

At last Thomas fully understood what it was to be a donkey. It was no light matter. His business in life was to carry anyone, whatever his mistakes, fears, or mischiefs, and he took a pride in doing it well.

And at last he understood how, as so many times his donkey had saved him, he must now save his donkey. He put an arm round the strong grey neck and said, 'We regard it as an honour to be counted among the donkeys. We have made a good journey.'

The donkey at once gave him a look of the utmost contempt and went away and ate thorns.

'What have I done?' said Thomas in bewilderment.

'I think he means we haven't made a good journey,' said Aubery. 'What have we forgotten?'

'*Oh*,' said Thomas, and for once his head bowed under the thought. 'My contract was to take Brother James back again.'

'And not only Brother James,' said Aubery. 'Have you forgotten the diamond?'

XX

For three days Brother James lay in the tent, his eyes composedly regarding something invisible to them on its roof, his voice clear and decisive in issuing instructions about his Eastern tisane, only his fingers looking strange as they tapped and plucked at the blanket in some frantic game of their own. Aubery inclined to the theory that the incorporeal spirits in the desert had given him bad news, but Thomas said no. 'They told me he was doing all the talking himself.'

But he was mending. On the fourth day he moved out of the tent, and took to spending the time striding round and round the camp: a sensible way of getting back his strength, if he had not stared in front of him and all the time muttered too low for them to hear. On the morning of the sixth day he emerged from the tent at mid-morning and announced, 'Tomorrow is the day we go East.'

Thomas was working on his store of leather goods for barter, while Aubery, cross-legged beside him, played a long formless tune on his Hliakh-pipe. Thomas said awkwardly, 'Yes, our stores are getting low. But we have news for you first, Brother James.'

As if he had not spoken, Brother James went on, 'And first I have to tell you my news. There is no such person as Prester John.'

Aubery uttered a snort that might have been laughter. Thomas, blinking, said mildly, 'Did you hear this from the spirits in the desert? Because I talked—'

'Spirits? I have talked to no spirits. I did not need to talk. This is a truth I have perceived; it has become clear to me.' A shade of uncertainty flickered over his face. 'I connect my growing clarity with–with this pain in my knee; which concentrated my thoughts. It is plain to me now that the legend of Prester John is one more example of the decline of the West.'

Thomas and Aubery exchanged baffled glances.

'Western Christendom,' said Brother James oracularly, 'has failed to save the Holy City. It has failed to keep the peace within its own boundaries. It has destroyed the great city of Byzantium. Its time is at an end.'

A dangerous look was coming over Aubery's face. He asked sharply, 'Do you propose then that we should desert it?'

'We shall re-found it,' Brother James said simply. 'We shall go East to Cathay and convert it to the true faith. We will raise the Church of Cathay. In the future, a true Prester James may ride West at last to rescue the Holy City. But for the present, we must apply ourselves to the founding of our new church.'

Aubery shouted, 'A *new church*! You brought us half over the world to found a *new church*?'

Brother James slid disconcertingly back into his old self for a moment. 'You wanted to see half the world, I think.' Aubery stamped in fury and turned away. Becoming abstracted again, Brother James added, 'The foolish story about Prester John brought our Crusade East, so it did us no harm. Tomorrow we march.'

125

'Yes, tomorrow,' said Thomas. 'Aubery, come and sit down, please. Brother James, that is your view as a—as a pilgrim. I am a Traveller. My view is different.'

'You undertook to guide me to Cathay.'

'No. I am under contract to guide you in search of Prester John, and back to Antioch.'

'I may go back to Antioch later; when my church is founded and secure.'

'Then,' said Thomas, 'I am under contract to return to the Sieur de Cahagnes his letter and his diamond.'

Though they might try to soften it, there was nothing more to say.

In silence, with the donkey looking on, they divided the stores into three equal parts. In silence Brother James put his own share on to his bedroll and looked at Aubery.

So did Thomas. With an effort he said, 'You made no contract, Aubery; you are quite free.'

Aubery went angrily red, stared at the ground, and kicked his share to lie beside Thomas's.

Then they all looked at the donkey.

The donkey swung his heavy head to regard Brother James from his deep-lidded eyes. Then he took his station behind Thomas.

Thomas found that he had not even been frightened of losing his donkey. His donkey was a Traveller.

It was a relief that Brother James refused supper and retired into the tent. Thomas and Aubery applied themselves to the last jobs before moving off; they spoke little, and then with great politeness. None of them slept much that night.

In the morning Brother James dipped his thorny head to take off the amulet holding the letter to Prester John, and Thomas dipped his sandy head to have the thong slipped over it.

'Greet from me,' said Brother James, courteously assuming their successful return, 'my cousin of Cahagnes and the Abbot, and beg them to remember in their prayers the church of Cathay.' As parting gifts he gave them two little packets, one of feverfew and one of a balm that healed open wounds.

'A fortunate journey and a good end to it,' said Thomas in a

Travellers' phrase (which avoided prayers), and gave him a handsome figured blanket-strap he had been working on for some time. Aubery simply looked miserable and held out his Eastern pipes.

'I have little skill with these,' Brother James said dubiously.

'A church needs music,' said Aubery. Pleased by the thought, Brother James tucked the pipes into his bundle, made the sign of the cross, and turned away. When he had taken three steps he turned back to give them another small packet.

'Since I am going East where it grows, it is only just that you should take my share of the Eastern tisane. I have kept enough for my supper tonight.'

And, his gaunt figure humped by the bedroll over his shoulder, he strode off into the glowing haze that was the Eastern horizon.

XXI

One thing in these later days Thomas found a relief, and that was that Aubery had returned to using his Western pipes. He still had some spare stems, but made no effort to turn them into another set of Eastern pipes, and when Thomas remarked on this said only, 'I don't feel like using them when we're going Westerly.'

He added later, 'I'll need them if we join another caravan. Time enough to make them then.' He did not ask if they would join another caravan; he knew now without telling that they would take what the road brought them.

He played a good deal now; it filled the silences when there were only two voices speaking. One day when his moody fingering of the pipe had failed to give him any tune he liked, he said, 'I suppose we shouldn't sing *Jerusalem* any more?'

'No. Well, we haven't sung it much lately.'

'No. What do you think we should sing?'

They had failed and they were going home: there seemed to be no Travellers' song for that. 'You'll have to make some up.'

In the next few weeks Aubery produced several. Some of them were unsuitable, like the one that started *Farewell and adieu to you, church of Cathay*, and another, with a good tune that Thomas found oddly familiar, and the refrain *Bless you, young woman*; Aubery said it was about an inhabitant of Cathay who got converted, but after hearing several verses Thomas forbade it. Aubery sulked at this, saying that some of them were very witty, and refused to play at all until they started climbing into the clouds. It was not a great climb, like some they had done, but it was a wetter one than any. Day after day the heavy mists veiled the hills around them, and rolled down on them and drenched them, and lifted only to show the next blue-black storm ready to move in. To keep one foot going after another Aubery came up at last with a relentless rhythm to which he set words in kitchen-French: *En passant par la Mongolie Avec tous mes frères*. It had a short verse, in which it was easy to improvise weary comments on the weather, and they sang it every day. Only at the end of the day did they come back to the Travellers' Song, suitably altered:

> *Just the clouds in the sky,*
> *And the mist around,*
> *No stars, no sun,*
> *But the mud on the ground,*
> *And you, my brothers, and I,*
> *Just you, my brothers, and I.*

'I refuse to believe,' said Aubery one night, huddling himself over the effort to kindle fire in the clinging dampness, 'that we were ever short of water.'

Their clothes flapped heavily around them, their sandal-thongs chafed and hardened in the knots, and they thought themselves lucky to achieve enough fire for a warm meal and drink; drying themselves was not possible, and daily they expected to see the sodden tent split into rotted strips.

When one morning Aubery's pipe proved to have so swelled in the wet that it would not play in tune, his temper broke, and with a curse he flung it far ahead of him into the mist.

'Let it go, Thomas, it's useless!'

But Thomas had started prudently after it, marking the direction in which it had flown, plunging into the mist, catching a glimpse of it as it fell and rebounded from a stone and tumbled again along the path.

Tumble? How did it tumble uphill?

Thomas threw himself on to the rolling pipe, secured it, and stood up, shaking the mud from his hands. He looked ahead of him transfixed.

'*Aubery! Ears!*'

Startled by the urgency of his tone, they came up to him at a run, and stood and stared.

Where they were, sunlight turned the mist into drifting streamers, shining at the edges with shifting and flickering rainbows. Ten yards ahead, the mist had gone. At their feet a clear stream ran chiming in a rocky bed, with grasses waving on its banks and cresses waving in its waters. Below them for mile upon mile rolled a vast golden plain of sun-warmed pastures.

They walked carefully and unbelievingly out of the mist to stand with the sun on their shoulders and feel it slowly warm them through their clothes. The donkey lifted up his head and methodically shook himself, ending at the tail, and the plume of water that flicked from the tuft at the end of his tail hung in the air as a brief rainbow.

'And I found your pipe,' said Thomas, laughing.

'And we'll need a new song when we're dry,' said Aubery, and skipped through the warm grass singing.

'What's that song?'

'I've just made it up. It's called—it's called—'

> '*Oh it's westering home and a song in the air,*
> *The long climb behind and a goodbye to care,*
> *West to our home and the welcome that's there,*
> *Land of our hearts, our own one!*'

'*The Westering Song*,' pronounced Thomas, and they padded down the soft grass singing it at the tops of their voices.

> '*Oh it's westering home in the warmth of the sun,*
> *Our backs to the East till the travelling's done,*
> *Friends in the West and a welcoming there,*
> *Land of our hearts, our own one!*'

'Because,' said Thomas, as the wretchedness of the last weeks fell behind them with the mist and rain, 'there *will* be a welcoming, Aubery! We've made the journey we contracted for, and it's a greater journey than any Traveller has ever made. What a welcome we shall get from the Travelling people!'

It was at this point that they saw the Mongol army.

XXII

They did not, of course, know that it was the Mongol army; but, spread over the miles of that vast plain, its numbers were so very much like the sands of the sea (than which there is no greater number) that they were never in very much doubt.

Both Thomas and Aubery made one movement to fade back into the mists, but the donkey, without a glance at them, continued his comfortable plodding downwards on the sweet turf.

'Even the donkey could be wrong once,' said Aubery, very pale.

'No, we're being stupid. Look, we're so far away that we can't even make out single riders, so they can't see us. And anyway they're on the move westwards.'

'Like us. And on the move they'll have scouts out all round,' Aubery argued.

'If they have them out all round,' Thomas said sensibly, 'they'll have them behind us. And we're only peaceful travellers.'

'Do armies recognise such?' Aubery objected; but sighing fell in behind the donkey, and they resumed their peaceful downward jog; though they did not sing again. They were still a thousand feet above the flat lands, which lay below them green and sparkling with tiny water-courses. Miles farther West, clouds of moving black covered the green, and at the limit of their view the clouds united into one great dark mass.

'I think,' said Thomas after studying this, 'that there, where they are thickest, is the end of this range of mountains, and that they are moving West through a broad pass just out of sight. Look–that must be a scouting party reporting.'

A wisp of black, like a cluster of bees rejoining the swarm, melted into the main mass and was lost. Farther back, another wisp flew out.

'Their speed!' muttered Aubery. 'No infantry there; all cavalry. And Thomas–*where are they going?*'

Thomas said nothing.

They made only half a day's journey, partly from caution, but mostly so that they could spend the afternoon basking in the sun, and spread out their tent-cloths and blankets to dry. Aubery, capering like a child to be free of the flapping of sodden clothes, attempted to swim in the meandering stream that ran through the cresses beside their camp, but came out smartly, blowing and shrieking.

'It's snow-water, you fool,' said Thomas, stretched in the warm grass.

'It was worth it for the sun afterwards,' said Aubery, and threw himself down to dry in the warmth.

They were dubious at first about lighting a fire, but in such pleasurable ease could not deny themselves bread and cooked meat and Eastern tisane afterwards; particularly the tisane afterwards. In this wonderful land the wood was dry, kindled without trouble, and burnt with a minimum of revealing smoke.

Aubery said thoughtfully, 'We gave up hope of help for Christendom from Prester John; but what about help from the Mongols?'

In spite of the sun a chill crept over Thomas. 'The Mongols are not Christian.'

'No, but they're tolerant of all religions.'

'They demand complete surrender.'

'They don't massacre, like the Muslims.' Being just-minded, Aubery added, 'And like the Christians.'

Thomas thought, as he so often did for all his attempts to forget it, of the burnt bones in the Valley of the Seven Trees. Who had done that–Mongol, Muslim, or Christian? He supposed that he would never know, and he wondered if it made any difference. 'The water's boiling,' he said. He shook the black leaves into the bowl, poured the water over it and set it near the embers to draw. At his shoulder the donkey blew softly through his nose, and behind him some other animal blew also through its nose.

Aubery looked up, rolled free of the fire and was on his feet, his fingers feeling for the sling in his belt. Thomas rose more slowly and showed his empty hands. The situation was beyond slings.

The noise of the stream had masked from them the approach of a band of horsemen. They carried bows over their shoulders, and knives in belts, and had goatskin saddle-bags and quivers and baldrics; their saddles and tunics were sheepskin. They were pale men, black-haired, narrow-eyed and broad-shouldered, and, though one could not see a hand or a heel move, their shaggy little mounts kept perfect order.

Thomas said over his shoulder to Aubery, '*Greetings!*' He put his hands together in the international gesture and swept a glance along the front rank of the horsemen to find the leader. A squat man with bracelets?– he was grinning unpleasantly. No–there at the other side was a flash of colour under the sheepskin and some fine metal on the baldric. He swung round to it and made his greetings.

He got out the Mongol greeting, the pure Turkish, and two mixtures of Turkish and Arabic and Turkish and Persian that he had found useful. The horseman with the bracelets said something over his shoulder that brought a roar of laughter, as well as some disagreeable round-arm gestures. Thomas thought rapidly: The donkey wouldn't be happy with them, he hasn't the speed. He could find some farmer in this land—

And then a voice spoke above him. It spoke a pure Turkish, too articulated and precise to come from any Turk. It said, 'How long has your tea been standing, good traveller?'

Astounded, Thomas looked up.

The rider with the fine trappings was a golden man; his skin was pure gold, his long hair was black and worn in a smooth braid, and his eyes had long tight upper lids that would not open properly. He seemed to be laughing; and he was looking at the bowl by the fire.

'Most revered and all-powerful master of all the civilised world,' said Thomas, 'about two minutes.'

'Then we have no time to lose,' said the golden man. A narrow golden hand, with long silver nails, made a smooth gesture behind him, and the precise voice spoke in Mongol. The man with the bracelets made an objection, which was silenced by two brief words which made the riders laugh. Bracelets grinned and beckoned behind him, and the riders were off with a drumming of hooves and a shower of torn grass.

The golden man gently brushed a few blades of grass from his sleeve and spoke again in Turkish, seriously and courteously, though all the time his dark slanted eyes were full of ironic laughter. 'Since you are only two, good travellers, you will not have a cup for me. May I therefore invite you to take your tea in my own poor vessels, which have the single virtue of having come from the home of tea itself?'

And sliding down from his mount he took from its saddle-bag a wonderful little box of some rich red shining material. It held tiny cups of a dull gold metal intricately worked, three of which he laid out on a flat stone, sat cross-legged by it, and with a flowing gesture of the silver-nailed hand invited Thomas to pour out.

Hovering anxiously, Thomas said, 'If–if this memorable drink comes from the great lord's own land, it may be that there is some necessary prayer or ritual to be observed—'

'While the tea stews?' said the golden man briskly, and picked up the bowl and filled their cups. 'The only absolutely essential ritual on the march is to fill each cup as many times as possible, and to keep water on the boil to fill up the pot when needed.'

He drank, and sighed with pleasure. Aubery woke up from his astonishment to rake the embers together and put more water to boil.

The golden man loosened his tunic, showing beneath it a shirt of golden silk, and pulled a stone behind him to rest his back. Thomas asked, 'Has the great lord eaten? Our poor provender is not worthy of the tis— tea, but—'

'I have eaten. We eat very well in the army. But we drink appallingly. Since you are plainly men of refinement, or you would not be finishing your meal with this excellent tea, I will not offend your sensibilities by going into detail about what one drinks in the army. Oh, and forgive me! When effected by a patrol armed to the teeth, introductions tend to be incomplete. My name is Li Pao. I have the pleasure of the company of—?'

'Thomas and Aubery, of the Guild of Travellers, great lord.'

'Not a great lord at all, I assure you: merely the captain of a wing. I am delighted to meet members of the famous Guild. And as I have intruded myself upon you in the middle of the tea-hour, pray allow me to prepare the next pot from my own stores. Is the water boiling?'

From the wonderful little box he produced a smaller box. 'I have my own pot, but yours makes such excellent tea that with your permission we will continue to use it. The water . . . ? Now we have only to wait. And we have all eaten, but travelling rations leave something to be desired for the tea-hour, do you not agree? Thomas, if you would be so kind as to hand me that green box—'

This held some tiny cakes of a reddish colour, which were meltingly sweet and sticky. Aubery spoke for the first time, saying, 'Not dates?'

'Not dates,' Li Pao agreed, 'but not dissimilar; we call this *hung-tsou*. Please help yourselves. So admirably arranged is the army commissariat that it will be some time before my stocks are exhausted.'

'The box,' said Thomas, staring at it fascinated: 'this being painted on it–I've seen one like it.'

'Oh surely not!' said Li Pao with his silent laugh. 'That being is a dragon. You have seen another painting, that is?'

'Yes. No: not a painting but a piece of embroidery. It came, I was told, from Cathay.'

'Cathay? I believe I have heard the name. More correctly, it is the land of the Sung. You would not have heard of the Sung?'

He sounded a little wistful, and Thomas said apologetically, 'We come from very far in the West. Are there no such things as dragons, then?'

Li Pao filled all three cups as he considered the question. 'He is a rash man, do you not agree, Thomas, who would say that such-and-such a thing does not exist? Myself I have never seen a dragon; on the other hand, many artists of my people appear to be quite confident of what dragons look like; what can I justly assume from this but that I may have been looking the other way when the dragons passed by me? But forgive me, something troubles you?'

It was the donkey, who, after giving Thomas a hard stare for some time, had now come round behind him and kneed him in the back. 'Your mount,' Thomas explained, scrambling up.

'The truth is,' said Li Pao remorsefully, 'that I have become much too used to having five grooms seize my bridle the moment

I dismount; also, I am afraid, to possessing at least twenty mounts whom I do not know personally. Wind of the Steppes or Flower of the Utmost Snows, or whatever your name is, I apologise, and you are too kind, Thomas. You can take the bridle off, he's trained not to stray. These Mongols think of nothing but their horses.'

'Aren't you a Mongol yourself?' Aubery was surprised into asking.

Li Pao looked shocked. 'But possibly you know little about the Mongols? I assure you that you wouldn't get half an hour's intelligent conversation from any Mongol that I have ever met; and oh dear, what a terrible number I have met. No, I am a Chinese, of the great Empire of the Sung. That is–I beg your pardon!–the formerly great Empire of the Sung.'

They nodded; his rueful tone made the situation clear. 'The Mongols defeated your empire?'

'I fear so: some time ago, of course, so that it has become perfectly allowable for us to enlist in their armies, but it is not the kind of shock one easily gets over, even in the course of many generations. Mongol virtues are undeniable, such as immense energy and unquestioning obedience to their leaders, but they are nonetheless a barbarous people with an entire lack of intellectual interests–a combination which makes a career of conquest unavoidable, don't you agree?'

'Yes,' said Thomas. 'We have some similar people in the Western half of the world: called Franks. There are not as many of them, and they have very little unquestioning obedience to their leaders; so they have troubled lands, but not continents.'

'How good it is to accompany one's tea with intelligent conversation! I had never before heard of these people. How are they about religion?'

'Stiff,' said Thomas, after a pause to pick his word.

'The one thing one must allow to these Mongols is a certain amount of sense on that score. Good order and the prompt payment of tribute is all they demand from their conquered countries.'

'This we had heard. But if one were to go deep into their lands and attempt to found a new religion there? We had a friend who intended doing that.'

'You would like me to estimate his chances of success?' Li Pao took more tea to help him. 'Thomas, forgive me, but I must first of all question that it can be a *new* religion. The prophets are new, but the faiths are old.'

'Yes,' Thomas agreed dubiously. 'But I meant a religion new to these lands; and he meant to go East as far as he could, which I think would bring him to your land of the Sung.'

'Eventually, if he went East. But he would have to go a long way, and not many things are new to the Sung.'

'The Christian religion?'

'Christian,' said Li Pao, making four beautifully articulated syllables out of it: 'let me think. Ah!' He crossed two long hands at an angle. 'Those? Oh yes: those we have known for some time. If your friend is an experienced traveller he will find them sooner or later; and presumably they will welcome him.'

It was difficult to explain that this was not at all what Brother James had had in mind. 'Are they–are they a flourishing church?'

Delicately Li Pao said, 'I am sure they are excellently organised and firm in the practice of their faith; but *flourishing* I could not conscientiously say: no.'

'Well,' said Thomas after a pause, 'perhaps Brother James will improve that for them.'

He could not make it sound hopeful, and was surprised when Aubery broke into a hearty laugh. 'Thomas, did we mistake Brother James from the very beginning? Are we sure that all he really wanted was not to travel East?'

'If that be so,' Li Pao said cheerfully, 'he should be extremely happy. If we were to–if we could!–set off from this agreeable spot and travel to my celestial homeland, I calculate that it would take us several months. Since you have honoured me with your confidence about this friend, would it be impertinent in me to enquire your own further plans? And as I fear we shall have to part very soon, would it be self-indulgent in us to brew one last pot of tea first?'

Juggling the scalding bowl, Thomas said diffidently, 'It would be a great kindness in you to advise us, if it did not conflict with your duty as a soldier. We are under contract–this is the code of the Guild, as perhaps you have heard–we have to return to a knight in the far West. There are two great seas—'

'I have heard; though not travelled that way myself, yet. And two great rivers in a fertile plain—'

'We have to go farther north than the two rivers, and then West still through mountainous lands to a third sea.'

'A great journey,' Li Pao said respectfully as he filled their cups. 'And I fear I can repay your hospitality only by offering you the most discouraging advice. Do not follow the army.'

They could not but admire the discreet way in which he had indicated the route of the Mongol army. Aubery groaned, but Thomas, who had been coming to the same conclusion, nodded. 'It will exhaust the food and water ahead of us. I had hoped it would travel so much faster–and this looks to be fertile country—'

'Oh my dear Thomas, you are thinking in terms far too small. That contingent you saw on the plains ahead–*that* is a mere outlier of one wing of the main body. I assure you that I speak with authority. I am, as you may have guessed, no great soldier, but I have a modest talent for organisation, and hold my rank in the commissariat branch. I fear you must go south for a time. Not north; the main body of the army is to the north. Skirt this valley on this side and go over the mountains south. You will find no difficulty with the terrain for at least some time, the passes are low. Beyond that I fear I have no information–a fact which, without being indiscreet, I can point out should be reassuring to you–but as you will most likely meet small foraging parties I shall be eternally obliged if you will accept this.'

It was a small tablet of what looked like solid gold, with odd characters engraved on it.

'Not one of the highest class of passes,' he said cheerfully. 'Those go only to the messenger-service, which would involve you in difficult explanations. This doesn't entitle you to free food or transport, but I see you carry the most sensible stores on the best possible transport, and at least it will permit you to travel without question. No, please don't thank me, but if you would be so kind as to catch that supercilious Cloud of the Last Lone Rock, or whatever he calls himself, I would be most grateful.'

Probably because he was not a Mongol groom, Thomas had difficulty with Wind, or Flower, or Cloud, and had to agree that he was a supercilious beast; but the donkey soon dealt with him.

137

'And may we,' he said as he brushed the mud off his quarters and led him up to be mounted, 'ask you to accept–I'm afraid we carry little of interest or value with us—'

They took care never to be left without a gift, and from all the people he had seen on the Crusade he had learnt some good variations for his more elaborate belts.

'But what accomplishment!' said Li Pao, delighted. 'If I had known that you were a master of this craft we could have talked at greater length. I shall be happy if you will accept in return—'

'You have given us the pass.'

'That was not personal. Oblige me by accepting this small but interesting box. You will see that it is decorated with the dragons you were interested in, and it contains, besides three cups, what we call a tea-pot. You will observe that the pot has a lid, with a spout for the egress of the tea. Your tea could not be faulted, but in a pot I think you will find that it retains its warmth longer.'

Thomas repeated the correct ritual of thanks; but when he made way for Aubery the boy abandoned them half-way to say, 'May I ask you a question?'

'Please,' said Li Pao, his eyes almost disappearing in his smile.

Aubery must have been revolving this for some time, for he had worried it into fair Turkish. 'I think you believe that the dragons of the Sung are legendary. We have been looking for a great king of our religion who has also turned out to be legendary. Why do you think people invent these–lies?'

Holding in his fretting mount, Li Pao said happily, 'Thomas, what a philosophically inclined friend you have, and what interesting conversations we could have had on this subject! But Aubery, I do not wholly agree that a legend is a lie, do you? About dragons, I hold by my first remark, that possibly they may have existed, though equally possibly not in precisely the elegant and imaginative form in which our celestial artists have depicted them. I have, for example, seen charming winged insects, no longer than my finger, which might very well have served for models–allowing generously, as one must, for the inspiration of the artist. As for your great king, would I be right in assuming that his existence was comforting to the imagination of your people in times of hardship? Then do not let us criticise. Comforting a fellow-man is one of the most meritorious actions in life.'

And with a flourish of hooves and torn-up turf the supercilious Wind or Flower or Cloud was allowed to go.

They watched the figure as it dwindled into a black dot on the green pastures. Long before that a cloud of other figures had whirled up to surround it, and all of them dwindled farther into something like a drift of smoke driving over the far plains.

After a time Thomas said, 'I think you may be right about Brother James. It's nice to think that there is still plenty of the East for him to explore.'

'Just as long as he finds a friend like Li Pao,' said Aubery. 'Well, Southerly. It's a beautiful pot he gave us, Thomas, but soon we're going to run out of tisane. No–tea.'

When they came to pack up, they found an oiled-silk bag full of tea where Li Pao had been sitting.

'Southerly. Away from all landmarks now,' said Thomas.

Aubery suddenly hit him spiritedly across the shoulders. 'Aren't we Travellers?' he said.

XXIII

Not only did they have to go far South to avoid the armies; before long they had to turn East again, for the countryside had been stripped of food. It was a bare bitter hill-country, and a bare bitter journey through it, where they did not dare choose an easy path. They saw no one; if there were men left alive, they took care to stay hidden. They were very high by the time they judged it safe to turn West again–or should it be South still? They discussed it tiredly for a couple of days, and then found they were wasting their breath. The lie of the land, with keen-edged mountains and ice-choked canyons, allowed them to go only one way, and that mostly South–South with a bit of West in it.

'At least if it's South,' said Aubery, beating his arms around him, 'it may get warmer.'

It got warmer very fast. They dropped down by tiny paths into forest valleys where no breeze could penetrate to blow away the stifling heat. When these valleys opened out, it was into evil-smelling black marshes, full of entrapping roots in the mud, and sliding snakes, and, worst of all, flaccid black water-slugs that fastened on flesh and had to be prised away, leaving behind them bleeding tears on the skin. Absurdly, in a place that seemed to hold more water than air, the donkey, who was particular about what he drank, suffered seriously from thirst. After a time they discovered a bush with large cupped leaves from which, with persistence, they could collect half a skin of water. Persistence took time; they got slower day by day. But when you are skirting the track of an army whose numbers are as the sands of the sea, with ten times as many horses, it is of little use to be impatient about your progress. Thomas, nevertheless, grew uncharacteristically worried. In his blankets at night he would repeat, 'Once we're out of this swamp—we can't do anything until we're out of this swamp. After that—'

'Well, what after that?' said Aubery, getting tired of his mutterings.

'West; West but with a lot of North in it. Someone—I forget, who could it have been?—someone went by the sea-coast—'

'Which sea?'

'But it was hard: too hard. He had ships too. Was his name Alexander? But there should be a way inland. I can't remember if I ever knew the landmarks, but there should be a way . . . Aubery, do you have to make the fire so hot?'

'Only to make you a drink,' Aubery said quietly. It was not tea, and Thomas tried to refuse it, but found that somehow he had swallowed it and was now drinking tea, but not in the same camp. In a confused way he started talking about their anxiety for Brother James and his knee.

'Ears, he's out of his mind,' he heard Aubery say, and then, very cross, began to rebuke him for making changes in the donkey's harness.

'There is no *need* for a donkey to wear a martingale,' he insisted.

'None whatever,' Aubery said cheerfully, pushing aside the branches of the swamp-trees for him. 'But since he is wearing it, you keep your hand on it and you'll find it easier to get along. I wouldn't swear to it, but I suspect that this swamp is changing.'

As everything changed, so in the end did the swamp. It did not seem an improvement to Thomas, because he found himself one day walking along a tiny causeway between endless floods, and was struck with guilt for having led his companions astray. But it seemed that he was wrong, because Aubery and the donkey had friends here.

The friends were in a tiny village on a rise in the ground, hardly more than a couple of feet above the floods, and the men of the village were engaged in the surely useless task of planting seedlings actually *in* the water, though most of them had given up work to crowd round Aubery. They were an exceptionally beautiful people, slender and swift, with skin-shades of blue-dun running into blue-black by the dark hair, which in the ladies surpassed anything Thomas had seen in all his travels, great ropes of glossy black swinging to their hips or great pinned-up knobs weighting their slender necks. Three of these ladies, the most authoritative having crispings of grey running through the black, took charge of Thomas, who somehow had lost all control of what was going on. They put him under a pile of coverlets in one of the huts and fed him noxious mixtures, which were unpalatable beyond anything he had ever dreamed of but made him sleepy. He tried on several occasions to get up and take charge of his party, but somehow was never successful, and presently decided that as these people were friends of Aubery and the donkey it would not matter if he had a short sleep.

It was a deep and refreshing sleep, except that numbers of people unkindly interrupted it.

Brother James, for example, would insist on telling him about the glories of the new Church of Cathay. 'I am very happy to know it,' Thomas assured him sincerely; but the gaunt figure continued insisting *Bells, Thomas, honest Christian bells ringing all over Cathay*, which worried him because he suspected that Brother James was ever so little exaggerating. A Crusading knight clattered by on a nappy bay, singing horribly out of tune, and a wild-looking creature who nevertheless played very sweetly on a pipe in the Eastern mode. One night they all began to crowd on him so fast that he could not identify them, which disturbed him; and, most terrible of all, there was one, quite silent, who simply stood in the shade of seven trees and never moved.

This night the three ladies of the house for some reason did not seem to go to bed, but were always looking in to see him, and often brought him cooling drinks, not all of them noxious. They did not speak any language he knew, so he addressed them at random, and they replied in their own language, and he learnt without effort their version of 'Lie back and drink this and you will soon go to sleep', and they appeared to learn too his version of 'You are very kind, but there are people here who are keeping me awake'. They sat by his pillow, and talked, and sometimes laughed softly, and sang curious featureless melodies, so that even though the intruding people would not go away it became difficult to hear what they said.

In the end, just before dawn, a completely new intruder arrived, a courteous golden man who bowed most elegantly and said, 'My dear Thomas, I am delighted that you have found such entirely delightful friends, not that I ever doubted your ability to surmount the troubles of a Traveller's existence, and do, when you can, convey my most friendly messages to Aubery and your charming donkey, as well of course as those of Star of the Final Snows or whatever he calls himself. My only reason for disturbing your well-earned rest is to draw your attention to the nature of the healing drink these hospitable and exceptionally beautiful ladies are now bringing you.'

For the first time Thomas took hold of the wheeling of circumstances around him, and recalled that the healing drinks had brought a familiar satisfaction. It gave him courage to look directly at whatever it was under the shade of the seven trees; when he saw for the first time that the only trouble there was that he had been refusing to take his medicine. He looked at the two cups the youngest lady was holding for him, and taking a brave breath drank off the noxious one; so that the presence under the seven trees vanished too, though not without a certain intensifying effect which he interpreted to mean that he must never be so stupid again. He looked at the second cup, smelt the steam rising from it, and said, 'Tea!'

The youngest lady, whose braid of hair he could not have encompassed in his thumb and forefinger, lifted her great black fan of lashes to look at him, blushed, smiled, and called the other ladies. It was quite easy to understand what she said: 'Come and see, he feels better!'

The other ladies ran in, chattered, laughed gently, shook up his pillows and shook down his coverlets, and the youngest one sat at the foot of the bed and in the sweetest voice he had ever heard sang a tranquil featureless song which sent him to sleep, he thought for weeks.

After that things were much less confused, and Aubery appeared at his side, an unfamiliar Aubery with his clothes belted high and long wet legs.

'I couldn't come before, Thomas. The women here only talk to the men of their own family, so it wasn't proper for me to come in. It was only proper for you because you were so ill. The donkey's very well and everything's all right.'

'We're eating their food,' Thomas said worriedly, 'and they don't look rich.'

'No, they aren't. They grow this grain, a new one to me, and barter it for everything else they need. But the donkey and I have helped with the planting, and the donkey's worked out a better method of getting the water on the fields. He's trying to work up a credit, so that we can take stores away with us. It will take him until harvest, so you've plenty of time to rest.'

Thomas was a little offended by the suggestion that he needed rest; but later the eldest lady explained to him that he had had a fever of the swampy lands, which would undoubtedly return, but that she could give him a herb which was powerful against it. They still had not found a word in common, but it did not stop them conversing. As Aubery had said, men here did not mix with women except of their own family, but his three ladies got over this difficulty by one hand holding the veil over the lower part of the face, which was a gesture only, even now when he was better, so that he knew their faces as well as he had known any face in his life. The middle lady had more laughter in her face even than Li Pao; but for beauty he thought he had never seen anything to equal the youngest lady, who was so shy that she seldom lifted the thick black fan of her lashes.

After some days he was able to emerge from the hut on to a balcony in front of it, and to his amazement found that the land for miles around was not a lake, but covered with some crop of the most delicate blue-green colour. Thigh-deep in the blue-green, among a crowd of men gabbling and singing, Aubery and the donkey were contentedly working.

Presently the donkey left the line and walked to the balcony. As if they respected the reunion, the villagers kept their backs turned and worked on. The sun shone on the blue-green crop and the blue-dun people, and in the hut behind them Thomas could hear the stifled laughter of his ladies and the pad of their bare brown feet.

'Oh Ears,' he said, 'this is a good place.'

Even the donkey spoke less coldly than usual. 'It is good. But what has that to do with us?'

Thomas sighed. 'It will be nice to remember it. Another two weeks, do you think?'

'Three,' said the donkey. 'It will be a long haul. Forgive me for being personal, but at the moment you look weedy. You should flesh up.'

'I'll try,' said Thomas, quite astonished by such consideration. He went back to the hut and obeyed; so much so that when at last, nearly a month later, he rolled up his blankets, he looked (for him) almost plump.

XXIV

It had deeply worried him, before they left, that he had no gifts for his three ladies. From this dilemma Li Pao once more rescued him, appearing to him in a dream to say courteously, 'My dear Thomas, those of us who have travelled as far as you and I from our homes cannot be ignorant of the ephemeral nature of possessions.' And if Thomas did not understand this remark in detail the gist of it was clear. Before he left the hut, he took Li Pao's dragon-box with the tea-pot and cups and presented one cup to each lady and the pot and the box to the eldest lady. The youngest lady looked as if she would have thrown her arms around him in pleasure, but instead was overcome with shyness and threw them around the middle lady instead. The middle lady looked sadly at him over her head. The eldest lady made him a stately speech, which he perfectly understood, and then made it even clearer by folding the box in her hands and holding it closely.

There was another fan of lashes outside to whom Aubery seemed to find it difficult to say goodbye, and Thomas thought it polite not to watch him too closely; though he was glad to observe that there was a kind of local nut which Aubery had learnt to carve into beads, and that the girl seemed sadly pleased at least with her necklace. The donkey, his saddle-bags well filled, took a path leading North-West, and as they turned every few hundred yards to wave the beautiful dun people faded into the watery blue-green dazzle of their fields and were gone.

'We have to make for a hill shaped like that,' said Aubery, drawing a complicated peak in the air.

'Why?' said Thomas, taken by surprise.

'It's the landmark. For the North-West passes. You said there must be a North-West way.'

Thomas could not think when he had said this. 'But surely the villagers didn't know it? They were farmers, not traders.'

'They said there was a trading-post five hours up-river, so I left the donkey to the harvest and went there, and there was a travelling tinker who told me the landmarks. He said it was a hard road but easier than by the coast.'

'Well!' said Thomas admiringly. 'You managed to learn the language, then? I'm afraid I didn't.'

'No,' Aubery confessed. 'It isn't like any language I've met. I just got on somehow.'

'If you want to, you can,' said Thomas, and they were both silent for the rest of the day.

The going was reasonably good, and the way, once they had climbed from the fields, quite clear to the Traveller's eye. Even Aubery, these days, could pick out the easy way across a small range of mountains. It was still warm, but would, the tinker had told him, get colder as they went higher, but not impossibly so provided they did not linger into the winter. That night, while Aubery was cooking their supper–he insisted on doing it because he said he had had lessons in preparing the succulent grains–, he said, 'That bag by your hand—'

It was a new bag, most beautifully embroidered, and he was at the same time deeply proud of it and trying to be casual. 'It was a present, though most of the things in it I earned or collected myself. Materials, I thought, for belts and necklaces to pay our way with.'

There were a good number of the carveable nuts, some skeins of coloured thread, some dried seeds in charming shades of pearl and brown, and some very useful leather.

'And this too?' said Thomas, holding up something from the very bottom of the bag.

'She wore it,' said Aubery, struck to the heart.

It was the richest thing Thomas had seen in the village. It was not very rich. It was an elaborate necklace of coloured seeds and threads, designed to show off its centrepiece, an irregular disc of silver a little larger than a thumbnail.

'Supper's burning,' said Aubery, laid the necklace at his side and shook the mixture of grain with herbs and vegetables into their bowls.

'Very tasty,' said Thomas as they ate. 'And I think it a very good idea, to make belts and necklaces. You will have to show me how these nuts carve . . . Aubery, I'm sorry; but may I see that piece of silver?'

'Why not?' said Aubery nonchalantly, and passed over the necklace.

Thomas took it on his palm. It looked irregular, but that was because it was heavily worn. He thought it had once been circular, and on either side he could see the remains of a pattern. 'A coin?' he said hesitantly.

It was something of a relief to see the Traveller's sparkle of curiosity come back into Aubery's preoccupied face. 'Other families in the village had them. All I ever heard was that they were very old, and had once belonged to some great king.'

The pattern on one side they could make nothing of, unless it were a figure holding out something in a hand. On the other side—if you thought of it as a head crowned with a wreath, you could see it so: and there were the remains of letters. 'We don't know the letters of these parts,' said Aubery, dashed.

'They aren't the letters of these parts,' said Thomas, staring. 'They're the Greek letters. That's a lambda, xi–*lexandr*– *Alexandros*: Iskander.'

'A great king who really did exist,' Aubery said with a sigh.

In one way, Thomas concluded as they made their way North and West, the stay in the village had done Aubery positive harm; and that was in the way of music. He had acquired another pipe, and also, not new songs, but a whole philosophy of music. One did not now have tunes; one had improvisations on peculiar scales, and somehow the improvisations had to change with the hour of day–a not very practical arrangement in travelling. Thomas did his best to follow, but when one day Aubery let slip that the improvisations should last several hours he gave up. Aubery then sulked, emerging only now and again to pronounce views on the origin of the universe, a matter which seemed to be bound up with music. It seemed highly likely that they were heretical views; but as they could have been communicated only in sign-language Thomas could not believe that they were a danger to Aubery's salvation. The music, when they had time for it to develop, had a curious hypnotic power, but what was the use of that? They had left that land behind for ever.

In every land that Thomas had known or heard of, there had been the saying, in one form or other, *This too will pass.* Travellers, naturally, put it differently; they said *We shall pass through this too.* They passed through the music of that land; they passed through the mountains; they passed through the kind (but lengthy) green plains that came after that. They passed with careful inconspicuousness, taking the small trails that ran from village to village, keeping away from the broad roads that joined town to town, not announcing themselves as far-Travellers, offering their belts and necklaces, or a day's labouring, for a night's lodging and a few days' stores. It was an inhabited and lively land, very fertile but with much busy trading going on. The people were sturdy and handsome, with bronze skins and much curling black hair, and most of them spoke a kind of Persian; they were fond of ornament, and, once Thomas had learnt not to stint on the flourishes, their leather goods had a ready sale. In one village they dosed a child with feverfew, and found that its father was a metalworker, who gave them a bag of studs and rings and buckles that were very useful. They also got, from a widow in whose house they stayed to do some repairs that were too heavy for her, some clothes dyed in the local colours. By noting the local ways of knotting belts and headcloths they were able to look not unlike local traders.

Aubery objected to this, saying, 'You've never worried about safety before, and these lands are peaceful.'

'They're prosperous,' Thomas corrected, indulging in his new habit of looking sharply around as they marched. 'And all the time we are going North and West.'

'Are you still thinking of the Mongols?'

'Yes.'

'I've been thinking about them too.'

'Thinking what?'

'That army we saw: that army could scatter all Islam if it wanted to. And Christendom is fighting Islam too, and the Mongols are tolerant of other religions. I don't see why Christendom can't ally itself with the Mongols.'

'Don't you?' said Thomas. He hugged his arms round himself as if in anguish, but said no more than, 'That is not for us to decide; and I thank heaven for it. But Aubery, I feel–I feel—'

'Feel?' said Aubery in surprise.

'Yes. I can't explain it. I feel that this land is not safe. I want to pass through it quickly.'

'Well, good,' said Aubery, who was inclined to grumble at their detours.

Was he, Thomas wondered, getting foolish? He asked the donkey one evening, 'Am I getting old before my time?'

The donkey said without hesitation, 'No.'

One day when they were skirting a village Aubery had declared they could find lodging in, Thomas said, 'We've never yet met a Mongol.'

'Li Pao.'

'He was a Chinese.'

'I had forgotten . . . Li Pao's escort we met.'

After that, Aubery grumbled less.

The countryside seemed to Thomas to grow less prosperous. One day there was a village that was not prosperous at all; it was a heap of smoking rubble, with evil birds hovering over it. Because they saw movement, they went into it; but found only an old woman who shrieked curses at them, so that they passed by quickly.

Was it their imagination that these signs increased as they went

North and West? One day they found a village that was entirely deserted; some dogs snarled from corners, but otherwise there was not even a draught-ox left. Past it a body of horsemen had left their tracks. Three days later they would have been surprised to find a village that was not deserted. 'We should get off this road,' said Aubery uselessly, for it ran through a narrow defile, and was cut up with hoof-tracks. They managed to find wandering paths at the edge of thickets, and at nightfall hoisted themselves into a well-hidden camp where they had shelter and water and could lie up for as long as they needed. But how long would that be?

Next morning Thomas said, 'Take your sling and get some of the birds that fly here, but stay out of sight. I'm going on ahead.'

Aubery, the new confident Aubery, clutched at him.

Thomas disengaged himself. 'I'll come back.'

To comfort himself, Aubery said, 'Look, the donkey isn't even troubling to say goodbye.'

All day Thomas slid and scrambled on little local rocky paths. It was not until the light was fading that he saw ahead a rise that would give him a view at dawn. He could not climb it in the dark, but pulled his blankets around him, munched the food he had brought, and fell asleep uneasily.

In the morning he woke and began to climb.

It was fair weather, which in these parts meant a thick mist, which would clear as the sun rose. He marked his high point, and cursing the rocks under his hands and knees approached it with caution.

He heard Christian bells.

He heard honest Christian bells calling to church.

He forgot the rocks, threw himself forward, and lifted his head over the skyline.

Below him were square miles of ruin.

In the pearly light of the morning a great city lay below him, levelled to the ground and burnt. The mist was not mist down there; it was the idle smoke rising from a slaughter-house, and he choked as the light breeze blew it into his face.

Among the ruins only one building stood unharmed. It was a steeple.

XXV

He made his way somehow back to the neighbourhood of Aubery's camp, and the donkey found him and guided him the rest of the way.

Aubery took the news hard. 'The *Mongols* sacked the city?'

'It's Baghdad. Sacked and burnt.'

'They don't sack.'

'They do if they are resisted.'

'But they left a Christian church unharmed? *Why?*'

'There was that queen who was a Christian. Perhaps they still have a kindness for Christians.'

'*Kindness!*' said Aubery on a sob.

It took all the efforts of the donkey to move them on: a long long circuit round the death and burning of Baghdad, and then away North, with a bit of West in it, but not so much that they remained in the trail of the Mongol armies.

There was no song left to sing but the Travellers' Song.

> *Just the path underfoot,*
> *And the sun in the sky,*
> *And you, my brothers, and I,*
> *Just you, my brothers, and I.*

They seemed to themselves to have sung it across the breadth of the world, and the days were long past when they sang it aloud with no fear of being heard. They took minor paths now, made long detours to avoid populated places, and went hungry when they might have looked for work or trade or hospitality along the way. 'I'm going to forget this country,' said Aubery spitefully. 'We haven't seen a friendly face for months.'

Soon they did not see any kind of face, for they had crept up into the mountains, savagely toothed mountains whose ranges seemed to have been crumpled and wrung and piled up beyond all nature, so that it taxed even Thomas's instinct to find them a way through. The paths dissolved into streams or crumbled into shale; above them hung the skeletons of old snow-drifts; sometimes the clouds sank below them and for a bare hour they saw great blue peaks shining above in a tranquil sky, and were too weary even to enjoy the sight. At night they huddled all three close together, clouds of breath smoking around them, nothing in their minds but the need to get the last warmth from the last charred ember. One night Aubery lifted his head and shouted at the peaks of Asia that were trying to blot them out, '*I am tired!*'

'We'll make a short march tomorrow,' Thomas offered.

'We will *not!*' Aubery shouted at Asia. 'We will make a *longer* march tomorrow; and then a longer and a longer! We *will* get out of this damnable cold!'

They made the longer march, sweating gasping up to a high pass. Aubery sang all the way, stubbornly and raspingly and with a rising high note of defiance; until at the last few yards the song was buffeted from his lips and he had to catch at the donkey for balance. The pass left them open to a great wind laden with snow that was sweeping from the North. They groped their way back for a sheltered camp-site, but the wind pursued them. As they threw the cloths over the tent-frame, the snow piled on it and the gale sucked at it, and, however often Aubery plunged into the storm to scoop the snow from the roof, the frame curved more ominously. 'I can't hold it!' he shouted against the howling of the wind. Thomas threw himself on the central pole; the seasoned wood cracked against him like a whip, and flung him away; the tent-cloths cracked with it, and the shreds whisked up into the driving snow and vanished; the snow swarmed upon them and the gale shrieked and snatched at them. He had an instant's glimpse of Aubery, his arms up to shield his eyes, tossed away into the darkness, and heard his last despairing call:

'Brother Donkey! Look after Thomas!'

XXVI

'Yes, it's very nice,' said Thomas, pushing away the insistent spoon, 'but I've had quite enough now, thank you. And I don't think it's at all proper for a princess to roll on my bed.'

Russudan, Princess of Georgia, regarded him from extravagantly fringed dark eyes in a rose-brown face, and deliberately put her curling dark head between her velvet-shod feet and turned a somersault. Her brother George, watching her with the same eyes saddened by the weight of tradition, said, 'It's a custom in our family, Thomas. We have always had heroic queens. There was the great Thamar; and then Russudan, after whom my royal sister was named. Though perhaps that was not a good idea.'

His sister threw one of the silk pillows at him, but Thomas intercepted it. 'Well then,' she said, settling herself comfortably cross-legged, 'tell us some more of your adventures.'

'I've told you them all. I want your royal brother to tell me more about Georgian politics.'

'No, that's boring. Tell about the storm and how you got here.'

'I keep saying that I can't remember most of it. I just hung on to the donkey.'

'And then found the patrol—' Russudan prompted.

That was all but the end of the story, but Thomas recited obligingly: 'And I didn't know it was a patrol, but the donkey trotted ahead and they stopped when they saw him. And picked me out of the snow and brought me in. And I said—'

Russudan clapped her hands and the two children recited it with him: '*I had two friends. In the name of God, please find them.*'

'And they did,' Russudan went on fluently, 'and brought you up here, and took the donkey to the stables, and Aubery—'

'Went with the patrol; and that's that,' said Thomas. 'Now it's George's turn.'

'Dull,' pronounced Russudan, kicking.

'My royal sister should remember,' George said sadly, 'that her

152

royal namesake was defeated by the Mongols.'

'She was not!' said Russudan, sitting up outraged. 'She got very favourable terms from them afterwards.'

George had plainly been born with all the diplomatic instincts of the prince of a beleaguered nation. 'Yes, well, but not unfavourable to them. And we enjoy very cordial relations with them now, but it wouldn't be wise to presume on that.'

'Tell me, George: is it because you're Christians that you enjoy these good relations with the Mongols?'

George looked politely blank.

'I heard during our travels—'

'Thomas, do tell us more about them!'

'Yes, all right, another time. I heard, George, that the Mongols seemed to favour Christians.'

'I never heard that. I never really heard of the Mongols favouring anyone. Or anything. They are a very *simple* people, you know. They're only interested in conquest, I think.'

'In tribute too?'

'Well, yes, but only to finance more conquest. In fact, Thomas, I suspect that they don't know that there *is* anything else to be interested in. And certainly not religion.'

Russudan, who had been giggling to herself, kicked him and said, 'What about Cousin Maria?'

George said stiffly, 'The case of Cousin Maria Palaeologina was purely personal. Though perhaps, Thomas, that was what you heard of.'

'And the others. Tell him about them.'

George's face took on the haunted look of a child required to remember history. 'We are naturally related by marriage to the other ruling Christian royal families: Byzantium, Trebizond, Armenia, and so forth. We know, of course, that they are all heretics outside Georgia, but these are not times to insist on points of doctrine. When it was clear that the Mongols were a power to be reckoned with in Asia, Byzantium naturally attempted to establish friendly relations, and our cousin Maria was married to the Mongol Khan. Some of the family were scandalised, but the marriage turned out a personal success. Cousin Maria is said to have had both charm and intelligence. And I believe that some other Christian ladies–they of course were heretics—married into that family, and no doubt they protected Christians where they could.'

'Would there have been one of those ladies around at the sack of Baghdad?'

'Yes, a Kerait princess. I believe it was owing to her influence that anyone was left alive in that city. Its mistake was to resist. The Mongols quite simply wipe out those who resist.'

'Well,' Russudan said pertly, 'the Franks sacked Byzantium, didn't they?'

An expression of pain crossed George's solemn face. Ignoring his sister, he said to Thomas, 'But this proves my point. The Mongols aren't interested in religion. Though we have heard reports that some of them are converts now to Islam. Untrue reports, we hope. We use the Mongol power to counter-balance the Muslim.'

'Thomas looks tired,' said Russudan. 'I think he should finish his soup. The doctor says he needs more flesh on his ribs.'

'No. I do wish,' said Thomas fretfully, 'that I could consult my donkey. The doctor says it's too far for me to walk, but I could try.'

Forgetting politics, George peered out of the window and nodded to Russudan, who rolled over the bed, seized Thomas's hand, and dragged him to George. 'We knew you wanted to,' they said proudly. 'Look!'

The walls of the castle were so thick and the window so narrow that Thomas had to put a knee on the sill and lean far out. To his shock, an icy peak fifty miles away looked serenely into his face, and as he turned left and right a whole circle of them appeared.

'No, no, down!' said the children.

Walls of stone fell away beneath the window, ridges and pinnacles and crenellated towers. Far below lay a yard, a palm's-breadth of green in which was a finger-nail of grey.

'Oh Ears!' said Thomas, overcome.

Far below a tufted tail twitched.

'We brought him there specially for you to see,' Russudan explained when he was back in bed.

'You're very kind.'

'So you repay us by telling us more about your travels.'

'And you did say,' George added apologetically, 'that you

could help me improve my Arabic. I know it's very impure.'

'Yes, yes, I will, both. And then be kind again and find me Aubery.'

When they had gone he lay in a doze. It was comforting to know that he could repay the kindness of these handsome Georgians; and fluent tent-Arabic would certainly be a great advantage to George; but he felt a little uneasy as he thought how long it would take to perfect George's Arabic.

He opened his eyes to see another young prince smiling broadly at him from the doorway—possibly one of the elder brothers of the twins. The Georgians, being a slender people with pale skins and dark eyes and hair, favoured a certain over-richness in their dressing, and this young one had chosen shades of saffron and bronze, which in the fading daylight blazed magnificently. Thomas pushed himself up on the pillow and began the correct ceremonial welcome. The young prince gave a whoop of delight and flung himself on him with a hug.

'Thomas, you're better!'

'Aubery,' said Thomas, dazed by his splendour. Of course he had realised that the boy had grown from the shrimp they had picked up in Outremer, but into *this*?

'You're so grand up here,' said Aubery beaming, 'with princes and princesses at your pillow, and I'm nothing but a plain cavalryman, I can't come into these apartments without permission. I came once, of course, after the patrols had picked me up and thawed me out, and I did slip up secretly now and again, but whenever I was off-duty you were asleep. Eat more, Thomas, put some muscle on your bones!'

There was muscle on his bones; in the dusk he looked seven foot tall and broad in proportion. 'Off-duty?' Thomas asked feebly.

'Well,' said Aubery, mastery radiating from every handsome inch of him, 'Georgia has always maintained her position by the strength of her standing army, hasn't she? And as a new recruit I thought I'd better not ask to go off-duty early too often.'

'*Recruit?*' said Thomas.

'Well,' said Aubery again; he looked down at his own splendour, and suddenly grinned his urchin grin. 'I'm not much of a cavalryman, Thomas, and I'd be even worse but for the help of Brother Donkey. Their conceited little horses here are all flourishing heels and no opinions worth mentioning, and at the beginning I was more on the ground than I was in the saddle. So I took the bone-headed beast I was supposed to ride over to Brother Donkey and asked him to have a word with it.'

'And what happened?'

'The donkey asked me to go discreetly away for a time. When I went back, he told me that the first owner of Little Bone-Head had had heavy hands, and that I might get some sense out of him by being lighter on the rein. He was being tactful, because when I groomed Bone-Head that night I found a lot of new mud on his back-side, and we get on pretty well now. I got recruited, you know, because of you and the donkey. You two got here by way of a pass they had decided was inaccessible. When the donkey proved that it wasn't, they needed me as a guide. Ouf!–trying to cram Little Bone-Head up rock-faces we'd come down feet first! But your eye for the land turned out to be right in the end, and they were so pleased that they adopted me as their scout. Well, I had to earn my keep, didn't I? I don't know if anyone's explained the political situation to you, Thomas, but I'm sure they're on the right lines.'

'Which lines are those?' Thomas enquired with reserve.

'They are in alliance with the Mongol governor in these parts.'

It was nearly dark now, only the fire in the brazier casting long lines of dull red light across the floor. Thomas said, 'As I understand it, they are vassals of the Mongols.'

'Oh no!' said Aubery with certainty. 'The treaty dates from Queen Russudan's time. And if anything can defeat Islam it will be an alliance of Christians and Mongols. So the real centre of the battle against the infidel is here in Georgia, isn't it?'

After a long time Thomas said, 'I saw the donkey just now. He wasn't wearing his girth.'

'That's safe,' said Aubery. 'It's with my kit in my quarters. Do you want it now?'

'I have the amulet with the letter,' said Thomas, 'and they belong together.'

Very clearly he remembered the figure of Brother James, stalking gauntly off alone into the mist of Cathay.

'I'll bring it when I can,' said Aubery; 'but we're on manoeuvres all next week, so don't worry if I don't get up here for a bit, will you?'

The donkey said, 'How do you do?'
Thomas said, 'A little shaky from getting down all those stairs, but on the whole tolerable, thank you. How do *you* do?'
'Thank you, very well. The grazing is thin, but they supplement it well. As you see, the poverty-line has disappeared from my flanks, and my ribs are well rounded.'
'I need advice,' said Thomas.
'Yes,' said the donkey, 'I thought you would. And I have given it consideration.'
'Thank you. I know,' Thomas said apologetically, 'that I'm slow. Anyone else who had travelled so far would probably have come to some sort of conclusion; Aubery seems to have done; but I'm afraid I haven't. All I've ever noticed is that politics and religion so seldom have anything to do with the really important things in life, such as doing your work and fulfilling your contracts; and I'm beginning to wonder if the really important people ever practise politics or religion. But somehow no one else seems to see it like that.'
'On the whole,' said the donkey, 'I do. But you and I are not going to alter the world with our opinions, so we had best be practical. It seems that there are two young ones of high birth in this castle who have become attached to you. If you wished to stay, the position of tutor would be open to you, and as I read the political situation it is stable enough for you to rely on passing the rest of your life here in peace. For me, the grazing is good enough. For Aubery, only Aubery can answer.'
'Yes,' said Thomas, who did not want to discuss Aubery, 'and it's very pleasant here and there is a good deal I could very usefully teach George. But you still think that we should just fulfil our contract?'
'Certainly. Why not?'
'Well,' Thomas said after a baffled pause: 'with the world in such a cruel muddle— And we did start off on a Crusade, which is supposed to make the world a better place—'
'Really?' said the donkey coldly.

'So is that all we can do, after so long and so far, just fulfil our contract?'

'I am open to suggestions. Have you any?'

Thomas was silent.

'The world is certainly in a cruel muddle,' said the donkey, 'but there would be a definite improvement in it if all contracts were fulfilled. A small improvement, so far as I am able to judge, but every little helps. However, you are not obliged to accept my advice.'

'Would I stop now?' said Thomas.

'I did not think it likely,' said the donkey. He sounded almost pleased.

There was very nearly a pitched battle with Russudan, who used her fists in her efforts to make Thomas stay, and a much more difficult time with George, who merely grieved quietly and attempted not to look his reproach. Since it was still too early in the year to set out, Thomas gave him a concentrated course in Arabic, with a little Greek thrown in, and taught him the correct words of welcome in every language he could remember. He spent many evenings making Russudan a necklace and bracelets in his most elaborate work. He explored the town, making friends and asking discreet questions; and one evening on the edge of spring (which here was heralded by a thunder of avalanches as the snows melted) went to a house in the lower parts of the town, where he was received by a plump dark-eyed lady with a brood of plump dark-eyed children running round her.

'Honoured Traveller, he'll be so glad to see you! But you will understand, please, if now and then he seems a little . . . Well, until we heard of your great journey he was the Far-Traveller in this city, and he feels it that he can't go on even the short hauls now with my man.'

'It will be an honour to meet him,' said Thomas, and presented her with gifts. There was such a plenty of everything in the castle that he had been able to save enough from his own share. She took him to an inside room where a one-legged old man sat with a stick beside him and a very suspicious eye.

'They tell me you've made great journeys,' he said.

Thomas sat down and began to talk. At the end of an hour they were on the best of terms, discovering like views and arguing fiercely about theories.

When he at last approached the reason for his visit, the old man said, 'Antioch?–no, I never attempted it. Too much local fighting. Nicaea I went to; and Byzantium many times, of course. But the political situation's bad for such a journey.'

'Have you ever known it good?'

'Eh?–probably not. But while all times are bad, some are worse. If I were you, I'd try the sea-passage.'

'Sea?' said Thomas. Georgia was about as far from seas as it was possible to get in these lands.

'Not the Soldaia route; those accursed Mongols use that. No, look.' With his stick he scratched a map on the floor. 'From here you can join the Westerly caravan. I take it you want to go quietly?–yes. Well, you leave that caravan–I can give you the landmarks; the summer's coming and there are good ways through those valleys. You make your way to the Western sea-coast. Not the big towns, mind!–you'll run into politics if you try that. No, you find one of the little harbours; they're all smugglers along there; make your own bargain with them. It would take you all the summer, of course.'

'I've taken so many summers now,' said Thomas.

Halfway through telling him the landmarks, the old man turned ill-tempered. He finished the landmarks, but even after Thomas's gifts of wine and honey his goodbyes were grudging.

'I'm afraid I've tired him,' Thomas said penitently to the daughter.

'No, Honoured Traveller,' she said. 'He's jealous; he wishes he could go with you.'

Thomas visited the donkey and said, 'Soon now.'

'I am in very good condition,' the donkey said graciously.

'Do you see Aubery at all?'

'If I take the trouble. The cavalry stables are open to me.'

'Then will you require him to bring me your girth,' said Thomas.

He had never before spoken so strongly. Next evening Aubery sidled into his room at sunset, all in beautiful shades of crimson.

'The donkey said you needed me.'

'Not you. The diamond.'

'I knew there was something.' Aubery hauled the old girth from his wallet. The buckle-stitching was just as he had done it, so long ago in the cellars of Belle-Désirée.

'Thank you, Aubery. The donkey and I are leaving tomorrow.'

'Are you?' said Aubery nervously.

'Are you riding better these days?'

'Riding? I'm a cavalryman. Every cavalryman can *ride*, Thomas. It's these confused valleys that trouble me now.'

'I hope you'll come to find them easier,' Thomas said politely.

'Thank you. I hope you'll have a good journey. Greet from me the Abbot and the Sieur de Cahagnes.'

'Shall I make your farewells to our brother?' Thomas was malicious; he knew that Aubery would not have the courage to say goodbye to the donkey.

'Please.' At the door Aubery turned, in a splendid blaze of sunset crimson. 'But Thomas—'

'Yes?'

'Thomas, the Mongols are defeating the Muslim all round. If we could make an alliance with them—'

'With those who sacked Baghdad? And,' said Thomas, at last making the effort because this was Aubery, 'the Valley of my Seven Trees?'

'Well,' said Aubery. 'Oh, I forgot: your gifts.' He had a new scarlet brow-band for the donkey, and a beautiful little bag for Thomas which proved to be full of tea. 'They get it in trade here. You always enjoyed your tea.'

Thomas was a little touched. He gave him one of his belts, with a wallet attached.

'And I thought,' said Aubery, 'that you might as well have this. It's of no use to a cavalryman of Georgia.'

It was the silver coin with *Alexandros* on it. Thomas looked from it to Aubery.

'I'm a *good* cavalryman,' Aubery said defiantly.

'I'm sure you are,' said Thomas politely. 'Good luck to you.'

'And to the two of you,' said Aubery.

XXVII

Caravan manners, Thomas noted, had declined lately. One or two impertinent youngsters actually asked him where he was going. The caravan master gave them a sharp word or two. He himself was a lesson in how things were changing in Asia. He called himself a Mongol, but had a golden face and black hair in a tail, responded with pleasure when Thomas gave him the greeting he had learnt from Li Pao, and then called the caravan to a halt for the Muslim hour of prayer. It was wiser not to enquire, but by a little watching and verbal nudging Thomas came to the conclusion that if the Mongols were conquering Islam in one way, Islam could be conquering the Mongols in another.

'And that's going to muddle their political alliances, isn't it?' he said privately to the donkey.

'It was to be expected,' the donkey said sombrely.

It only confirmed Thomas's view that politics and religion seldom had anything to do with the really important things in life. Here, for example, were they, on the really important business of fulfilling a contract, on the best of terms with a Mongol Muslim who was doing his job in life. They were, in fact, on such good terms that the Mongol Muslim, obviously used to the ways of far-travellers, took the trouble to give Thomas the landmarks for a short cut on to the road recommended by the old man in Tiflis. So, not many weeks after leaving Tiflis, Thomas and his donkey turned off up a side-valley and were travelling on their own again.

Compared with some earlier times, they were magnificently equipped. George had taken on himself the ordering of their stores, and had stopped adding to them only when the donkey could carry no more; then Russudan had tucked sweetmeats and small gifts into every corner; and at the last George had made a deeply formal speech and handed over five golden coins as payment for Thomas's teaching during the winter.

'Which means we need not stop to work for our keep on the way,' Thomas told the donkey. 'And if necessary, when we get to the coast we could pay for a sea-passage. We don't know what we'll find there, do we? The port for Antioch is Saint Symeon, but after that, do you know that I think I'll have to ask the way? Somehow I can't call it to mind as I should. . . . I wonder if the Sieur de Cahagnes is still there?'

It was the first time that this had occurred to him.

'I think he said he came from Frankland; perhaps he's gone back. We have been quite a time on the way, haven't we?'

He could not count the seasons back to that day when he had slipped quietly out of the side-door of the abbey, with only old Brother–what was the name?–to see him go. Winters in the marshes, summers in the high bleak plains, featureless marches when no one could have said whether the year was growing or falling— He gave up. 'At any rate our contract is clear. Back to Antioch, we said; so if the Sieur de Cahagnes is gone we can hand the diamond over to the Abbot. Oh, and the letter as well. That's of no use now, but they'll want to see it destroyed . . . And then what about us, Ears?'

The donkey did not even look at him.

That summer, in fact, the donkey was not talkative. There was no need for him to talk, because they were doing what they had to do; which was to cross the rest of the breadth of Asia. Looked at like that, life was simple and full of importance.

There was only one night that broke the good monotony of the journey. On a fair calm evening they came down to a ruined city by a long lake. It had not been ruined by war; it had been deserted, so long ago that down by the lake, where they made camp, the paving had been broken by sad willows that now hung dead and hollow among the stone shards. There were broad flights of stone steps broken and buried in myrtle and ivy, a double row of fluted stone columns that marched toppling and purposeful into a rabbit warren, and a great triumphal arch twisted and fallen in a grove of cypresses.

But all the ruin had been so long ago that it was a peaceful place. The donkey drank good water from a basin where the stone lip had been worn away by the dripping, and Thomas banked his little fire and lay back under the cool stars, and wondered as he fell asleep what fine soldiers had ridden in triumph under the arch. On the very edge of sleep it came to him that, if they had come in triumph to this fine city, they must have left another city somewhere sacked and burning.

Perhaps that thought pursued him over the edge of sleep, because he woke while it was still dark, his mind still full of thoughts of smoke rising from ruins, and in his ears the echo of some name, roared from a thousand throats. Perhaps the air over the lake had once resounded with that name; but now there were only the owls hooting across the silent water. The thought left from his forgotten dream was: But now he is as dead as the enemies he killed.

'Who? Who?' said the owls across and across the lake.

He sat up with a shiver and blew up the embers of his fire. Among the sparks was one that shone cold and did not die away when he stopped blowing. He shook the soil from it and rubbed it between his hands until the whole silver disc shone clear. It was not as worn as the one that had found its way into a girl's necklace in the South, and you could see quite clearly the head crowned with the wreath of victory, and round the rim the Greek letters for *ALEXANDROS*.

'Who? Who?' said the owl on the arch of victory.

And after due time, as happens in all good journeys, they came to the sea.

It was mosque country, but well cultivated and peaceful. They went openly, but quietly, by small roads, and finally found a rock-bound fishing-harbour where there was a bustle of sailing boats. It did not seem a place to show a gold piece, but there was a man whose camel had gone lame just when he needed his family wood-pile replenishing, so they did that for him in exchange for the promise of a passage along the coast, Thomas to supply his own food and help off-load at the other end. Where exactly the other end was to be the captain would not specify; but then Thomas had no wish to specify exactly where he wanted to go either. It was all very well to imagine landing at the port of Antioch, but, when they had left, the greater part of that coast-line had been in infidel hands.

They finished the wood-pile, re-packed their load and trotted down to the jetty. The boat was swaying gently in the swell, and Thomas looked at the sea beyond and knew that he was looking straight at Antioch and the end of their journey.

And then something happened that had not happened since the desert of the incorporeal spirits. The donkey looked over the sea towards Antioch, stretched out his neck, and said, '*Take care! Take care! Take care!*'

Then he set his four small hooves on the jetty and refused to move.

Thomas took little part in the battle that followed, being too much shaken by the warning, except to say to the ship's master, 'If my donkey doesn't mean to go, he won't go.'

'I never knew a donkey you couldn't say that of,' said the master, wiping away sweat with his forearm, 'but you can sometimes fool them.' Taking no notice of Thomas's mutter of 'Not *my* donkey,' he put his shoulder to the donkey's and shoved it hard away from his boat. To a lot of ironic cheering from the crowd, the donkey obediently backed away, swung round and picked his way along the gang-plank of the next boat.

There was a baffled silence.

The man who owned the favoured boat said hopefully, 'He's a strong worker, your donkey. You wouldn't be wanting to sell him?'

'*No*,' said Thomas. 'I see you're only half-laden. Will you give us a passage if we finish the job for you?'

'I'm not going south, you know.'

'That's all right,' said Thomas jadedly. He had no doubt at all that the donkey had this in hand.

He had to learn how to keep his feet in a boat, so that it was a couple of days before he was fit to notice directions. Then for once he lost patience with his donkey.

'*North*. And may I ask, Brother Donkey, what you think you're being so clever about? What are they going to say in Antioch when it gets about that Thomas and his donkey stole the Sieur de Cahagnes' diamond?'

Chewing steadily, the donkey merely looked at him offensively, indicating that he was not being very intelligent.

A chill settled on Thomas. Next day they beached in a hidden cove, and the master asked hopefully if Thomas thought of disembarking there.

'I've quite a load to be taken to the town, and my cousin keeps the inn there; he'd give you lodging in exchange for a bit of help.'

The donkey trotted nimbly ashore and stood to be loaded. Thomas politely refrained from enquiring about the contents of the bales, but as they kept to back alleys it was obviously something taxable. The cousin at the inn made them free of a corner of the stable, and, while they ate, a prosperous-looking man with two pack-camels came to share their hay-bale. He was a Muslim, a mountain of a man with a great red beard, and in spite of his religion he affably offered Thomas some peppery dark wine. 'How were the roads?' he asked.

'My last stage was by sea.'

'Never trust it. There are devils there who attack you in your most useful spot.' He slapped his imposing stomach. 'I'm last up from Southerly. Quietening down there at last, praise to the All-Merciful, so that a man can begin to go again about the really important things. Not that I had anything against the native Christians. They'd spend a day beating your price down, but once they'd made the bargain you could trust them.' He drank as if in a regretful toast to trustable old bargains. 'But they were never what you could call orderly, upsetting trade with their endless quarrels; and they do say that their prince had gone off to present his compliments to those murderous Mongols.'

'Prince?' said Thomas, almost voiceless.

'Something wrong, friend? Yes, prince–Bohemond of Antioch; *was* of Antioch, I should say, luckily. We couldn't have clients of the murderous Mongols right in our lands, could we? Though it was a good town. I couldn't see that it was necessary to— But it's done now.'

It was a few drinks later before Thomas could trust his voice enough to say, 'I have been far-travelling East and had no news. Antioch–the Christians—?'

'Well, the Christians,' said the red-bearded man: 'oh yes, there are still some around. Acre, you know, down the coast, and a few other strong towns; and I believe some of them cast up in Cyprus.'

'Antioch?' implored Thomas.

'Antioch,' said the red-bearded man uncomfortably: 'yes, well; I did say I couldn't see the need to—'

'Sack it?'

'Well, not quite so completely. I was there a couple of seasons after; still not a pretty sight, I'm afraid. Did you have kin there?'

Thomas nodded, speechless.

'They say,' said the red-bearded man consolingly, 'that the number of slaves taken was enormous. It was because of the Christian alliance with the Mongols, you see. You do see that we couldn't have that? You aren't well, friend. Try a good drink.'

Thomas looked at the wine offered to him. He found that he was counting at a great pace, as once long ago he had counted in the Valley of the Seven Trees; and choking, as once he had choked in the smoke rising from the ruins of Baghdad. Amina; and Hakim; and his godson, young Thomas; and Thomas's brothers and sister; and Brother Hadrian; and the Abbot, and the Sieur de Cahagnes, and Brother Hieronymus and—

He took a good drink. He said with difficulty, 'Thank you for your news and good company,' and fumbled his way around the stable until something under his hand became the strong shoulder of his donkey.

'Ears, oh Ears!' he said as he dropped in the straw at his feet.

The soft white nose of his donkey touched his cheek. As he fell into sleep, he seemed to hear an owl calling.

He woke to find the stable blue with dusk and his head aching horribly. Outside, the owls were calling, 'Who? Who?' He lay where he was and looked at the dark below the roof above him. There was a warm sweet breath on his face.

'As far as I can see, Ears,' he said, 'we have come to the end of our usefulness in life. What shall we do now?'

He felt the movement as the donkey swung his head to look through the stable door.

A lantern came in, held high to light the face of the red-bearded man. He was nodding and winking and signalling urgently with his eyebrows, jerking his head to Thomas to wake up and get on his feet.

Over his shoulder he said, 'Now this I really do guarantee is exactly the man you want.' His head came round and winked furiously again. 'A Traveller born, experienced on all the most difficult routes. I assure you you're in luck to find him here just when you need him. This gentleman,' he said to Thomas, frowning at him ferociously to take notice and brush the straw out of his hair, 'has had the misfortune of a shipwreck. I told him the sea wasn't to be trusted, and he has decided to take the overland route home. He needs a guide. I'm sure you can help him.'

And he stood back beaming and holding the lantern high, one Traveller pleased to introduce custom to another.

Because the straw in his eyes was making his headache worse, Thomas brushed it out. What had this to do with him?

With great deliberation, the donkey began to move; forwards, then broadside . . .

Thomas saw that he was in line with his donkey's hindquarters. He was on his feet in one movement, shaking off the straw.

The light of the red-bearded man's lantern fell on a thin-faced worried man in the rich dress of a nobleman, brisk and businesslike.

'Your name is—? Thomas-ben-Matthias, thank you. You are of the Guild?–thank you. I have an escort of six men, with ten good pack-animals. Our status is diplomatic, but we are carrying only personal goods. Is it true that you know the roads to the North-East?'

Thomas looked at the donkey. He saw only its hind hooves, shifting a little for good purchase. He looked the nobleman up and down, and his professional judgment awoke and took charge of him. 'No, my lord, I don't know them, but I can guide you if you can give me two hours to consult my fellow-members of the Guild in the town. You–have a contract for me?'

'If you wish one,' said the nobleman, worried. 'You look unwell.'

Thomas turned his eyes on the donkey. The donkey turned his eyes on Thomas, around his hind hooves.

'I wish one,' said Thomas. 'I am quite well, and a Traveller. May I know your name, and your destination?'

'My name is David Comnenus,' said the nobleman, 'and my destination is Trebizond.'

XXVIII

The escort, though well intentioned, were a barbarous lot, and during the long journey, which was no different from all the other long journeys Thomas and his donkey had taken together, the Most Noble David of the August Family of the Comneni, Born in the Purple, Chamberlain of the Imperial Palace, Count of the Imperial Guard, Keeper of the Imperial Seals, talked a good deal to Thomas over the camp-fire at night.

'All a deal of nonsense,' he said deprecatingly of his string of titles. 'The Comneni were an imperial family, back in the days when Byzantium really was Byzantium, and then in the time of the great disaster, when the Franks sacked the city, a couple of them escaped to Trebizond and set up what they called an empire there. They were related by marriage to the Queen of Georgia, and she gave them some help.'

'The great Queen Thamar.' Thomas nodded.

'I see you are a man of education. In Trebizond we have a good defensive position, but we are a very small domain, and all this imperial flummery is nothing more than an attempt to comfort ourselves.'

'Which is meritorious,' Thomas said, 'but should not be too much indulged in.'

'I must agree. Now I am merely a cousin of the present Emperor, and am a dull old scholar who was sent on this embassy because my scholarship includes an obscure Western language called Frankish.'

'I know a little of it.'

'It has its uses among the heretics of the West. Ah, tea! Delicious, Thomas, thank you. But it was a hopeless embassy. As well as heretical, those Westerners are ignorant.'

'Of what in particular, noble lord?'

'Of politics. They call themselves imperial, but do they take advantage of their chances of empire? Some time ago the Mongols positively sent them an embassy—we knew of it because it took ship from Trebizond; its task was to suggest that the

Christians of the West should join them in an assault on the Muslims. Did they take up that offer? Did they even stop to wonder whether the Mongols might not be more dangerous to them than the Muslims? No, and no. They have lost interest in Jerusalem except as a piece of sentimentality for hymns and sermons, and all they do is quarrel about their own domains.'

Thomas started to speak, and instead offered the Noble David more tea.

'Thank you, thank you. When we arrive, Thomas, remind me that I must make enquiries about this sustaining herb and renew your supplies; as well, of course, as starting a small trade in it myself. But surely you were about to make some comment on the heretic Westerners?'

'Only, my lord, that it is surely better to have the Franks quarrelling about their own domains than have them quarrelling about ours?'

'*Very* much better,' David agreed. 'The crusading fever is over, I trust, and perhaps here in the East we can have peace to fight our own wars . . . And what about you, Thomas? What will you do when you've fulfilled your contract with me?'

The donkey was not there to help Thomas; he sat looking into the firelight. 'I'm a Traveller by trade,' he said at last.

'You've surely travelled enough for one life-time,' said David. 'Travellers settle in the end, I believe? If you would like to settle in Trebizond, I should be most happy to assist.'

'You're very kind, my lord. I once saw Trebizond. I should dearly like to settle there. But I don't think I shall be allowed.'

'What should prevent you?' David said kindly.

Thomas could not tell him. The letter in the amulet was useless now, and he kept it only out of sentiment. But what was he to do with the diamond in the donkey's girth-buckle?

XXIX

'And hereby,' said the Imperial Herald, stepping back with a flourish, 'we, the Most Noble and August and Imperial Majesty of the Eternal Empire of Trebizond, with all our titles as aforesaid, do invest you, Thomas-ben-Matthias, here known as Thomas Far-Traveller, with this plot and portion in the street of our capital city known as the Street of the Golden Cockerel, with the garden and allotment pertaining thereto on the outfields of the city.'

The donkey bunted Thomas until he had put together the right phrases of acceptance and gratitude.

'Right,' said the Imperial Herald, briskly pocketing his ivory tablets, 'and I told them to start a fire for you, because I want to taste this herb drink of yours that everyone is talking about. They say there's a shipment coming in later this month, but it won't be cheap.'

Thomas got the tea-making equipment from his battered old bedroll, which looked very strange in the neat little hut, with the bright hearth and the stable for the donkey. 'But I never expected any of this. It was very kind of the Most Noble David to recommend me to his Imperial Majesty, but—I don't know what to do about it.'

'If I were you, then, I'd go out and take a look at your bit of land. Ask some advice from your neighbours about what best grows there. So this is tea? Yes, I think I must put my name down for some.'

Thomas and the donkey went out and looked at their piece of land, among the gardens and allotments in the outfields. It seemed foolish to leave it unplanted, especially as the year was just moving into spring. He owned no tools, but the donkey carted manure for a neighbour, who in return lent him a spade and a mattock, and then gave him seeds on the understanding that they could share the donkey when it came to taking their produce back to market. There was not so much as a stool in the hut, and Thomas was no carpenter; but then the carpenter down the alley was not much of a harness-maker, and in one way and another he and the donkey were soon pretty snug. There were friendly people in the Street of the Golden Cockerel; which (as tended to be the way in Trebizond) was not so much a street as an alley with steps every few yards; and if Thomas went outside his front door and put back his head as far as it would go he could see the towers of the citadel, blue-gold in the sun.

'Don't you miss the travelling?' Joseph (the neighbour) sometimes asked.

'Not really,' Thomas would say honestly. 'We Travellers do settle down. But only in the end.'

'It always seems to me that you might be up and away any day; as if there's something on your mind. If you ask me, it's the donkey that's unsettling you.'

No, it was not the donkey. The donkey was perfectly tranquil, and seldom had anything to say but the sharp reminder that his water was not fresh. It was the donkey's girth that was the trouble.

By the time of their second planting in Trebizond, all of his harness was new and well worked, made by Thomas as he sat by his bright hearth in the evenings; but the old girth remained as it was, as the boy Aubery had stitched it together. It was grey and rubbed now, and Joseph often wondered why Thomas did not replace it and make the donkey as smart as such a worker deserved; but Thomas always shook his head.

'You know what,' said Joseph, exasperated: 'when you replace that girth, I shall be sure I shan't come one day and find your hut empty.'

They were coming home one evening in the summer, their tools over their shoulders and a good load of vegetables for market in the donkey's panniers, when they saw the Imperial livery at Thomas's door. Thomas's heart sank.

'What's all that?' said Joseph.

'Joseph—if I don't come back, harvest the plot yourself, will you? And if you want your daughter-in-law to stay with the new baby, use the hut—the winter rugs are in the chest by the door—'

'I knew it. How am I to work both plots alone?' Joseph complained.

The Imperial Herald was a friend now—Trebizond was not

very big, and there were few people in it Thomas did not know—but for once he refused tea, hurrying Thomas away up the steps to the citadel, as much as anyone could hurry up the slopes of Trebizond.

'The Most Noble David?' Thomas asked between pants.

'No. Order from the Imperial Chancellor, so it came from the Emperor.'

Trebizond was not very big but very rich; Thomas was conducted through room after room hung with gold-figured tapestries before the double doors closed softly behind him and he was left in front of the figure of a tall old man in a dark gown. He called to mind the correct form of greeting for high palace officials, and had begun, 'Right Esteemed and High-Born—' when the old man said grimly, 'Well, Brother Thomas?'

It was Brother James, back from Cathay.

He was not Patriarch of anywhere; he was a Traveller, with his wallet on his belt and his old bedroll on the floor at his feet. Somewhere in the following confusion of Imperial officials explaining and pressing Imperial hospitality, the Most Noble David appeared, waving them off and telling them to let Thomas take his old friend home.

'It seems you have acquired a home,' said Brother James, gauntly padding down the alleys and steps.

'You'll like it, Brother James. And the donkey—the donkey will be so pleased to see you! How did you—no, you can tell me that when we get there; no one can talk in these alleys. Oh, just wait until the donkey sees you!' crowed Thomas.

The donkey looked Brother James up and down, nodded his heavy head, and went on with his supper. Thomas sat Brother James down, made the fire bright, rushed among his neighbours borrowing the choicest things they had for a grand supper, and brought them all crowding to see his travelled friend. They were impressed by Brother James, who sat austerely silent but nodded graciously to each introduction. The only time he spoke was when Thomas proudly announced that his friend was a healer, and someone behind stood on tiptoe to call, 'If my wife brought down our youngest that got the splinter in his foot, would the healer look at him?'

'If I am still here, I shall be pleased,' said Brother James.

They went at last, and as Thomas got out the bowls Brother James handed him an oiled-silk package. 'Tea,' he said: 'a different flavour.'

And, after all, there was not so very much to say. Brother James had been to the land of Cathay. It had been a long journey, though interesting. The people there had been much like other people, though more courteous and with golden skins and eyes that did not open properly.

'Yes, we met one,' Thomas nodded.

Brother James had learnt their language, which was more difficult than most. The Mongols were the ruling people there, and were not in the least interesting, thinking of nothing but conquest and horses. The golden people of the Sung, on the other hand, were cultured and most interesting, except that they could not keep their minds off the past. Whatever the subject of conversation, they would veer off to some great empire they had once had.

'Yes, empires have a bad effect on people,' said Thomas. 'Did you happen to meet any dragons?'

'In spite of my efforts, no. Many who had met them, however.'

'Did the dragons talk to any of them?'

'So they said. But all of it about the past.'

Thomas was not really surprised. With some trepidation he asked, 'And the Christians of Cathay?'

'Yes, there were Christians. The Mongols permit them. Perhaps a hundred in each city. The cities are far apart. It appears to have become doctrine in each city that the congregation there is Christendom and all congregations elsewhere heretical.'

That was all the explanation Brother James was ever to offer for his return from Cathay. Nor, on the whole, did Thomas ever feel that more explanation was needed. But he did want to know how Brother James had found them in Trebizond.

'As I came Westward,' Brother James replied austerely, 'I considered the question, and concluded that if you had your will you would be here. You like this tea, I hope. The people of the Sung have countless different flavours of the herb, all very subtle. They are a subtle people. And our brother Aubery?'

'Aubery had his will too,' said Thomas. 'There is a land called Georgia—'

'I have heard of it.'

'You passed through it?'

'No. But I heard of it as a land of warriors.'

'Yes. Aubery decided to be a warrior.'

'He was young,' said Brother James.

'You heard about the–the sack of Antioch?'

'You had kin there. I am sorry.'

'Thank you. So here the donkey and I have come. And here we still have the letter and the diamond. Brother James, what are we to do about those?'

'Make another pot of tea,' said Brother James.

They made it, and considered the problem.

'The political situation,' pronounced Brother James, 'makes it inexpedient to preserve the letter. I think it should be destroyed.'

'And so do I,' said Thomas, relieved. 'But I didn't like to do it alone.'

He took the amulet from his neck, and between them they watched the letter flare and fall into ashes in his fire.

'But the diamond?'

'What does the code of the Travellers say for such circumstances?'

'That the diamond, or its value,' Thomas said readily, 'must be returned to the man who gave it.' He was struck by an idea. 'Brother James, you're a cousin of the Sieur de Cahagnes. Couldn't you inherit the diamond, and give it to charity?'

In silence, Brother James worked it out; and shook his head. 'My cousin Reynauld had daughters; married, though I am ignorant of to whom. Their children–grandchildren?–are the heirs.'

'And they live in Frankland,' said Thomas. Must he take the diamond on another journey? The thought struck a pang to his heart; the trouble was, he did not know whether it was a pang of longing or a pang of terror.

'But there is trade,' said Brother James, 'between Trebizond and the West. I have heard of that already, and it seems that you have friends here. Could enquiries not be made?'

After thought, Thomas told their trouble to the Most Noble

David; who, it transpired, was engaged in a small trade of spices to the West, and readily undertook to enquire for the heirs of Sir Reynauld de Cahagnes. Since this would involve a long wait, Brother James had to be settled in Trebizond. They built another floor under the rafters of Thomas's hut, and prepared to share the work of the allotment. But so many people wanted to consult the new healer that Brother James had to explore the market for herbs and drugs; and in that way he came to know better than either Thomas or Joseph how to dispose of their fruit and vegetables. When the Most Noble David jogged down the steps one day to pay them a visit, he found Brother James a congenial companion, and made a note of the name of the subtle scented tea, in the hope of arranging for a shipment of it. But as for the heirs of the Sieur de Cahagnes, as time went on he had to confess that so far the search in Frankland had met with no success.

'There were only daughters, you see, and you have no ideas of their husbands' names. And of course records of those who perished in Antioch—and indeed in most of the rest of Outremer—are, well, lacking. I don't wish to enquire into your private affairs, Thomas and James, but unless it was a really valuable property you have in mind—'

'It's one very large diamond, Most Noble David.'

'Oh dear. Yes, that could hardly be disregarded, whatever the difficulties. Don't despair, dear friends. I will direct that enquiries shall continue. Meantime, you are quite comfortable here, I hope?'

They were very comfortable. It was a good season, and with the profit from the allotment they were able to buy new blankets, in the bright clear colours favoured by the weavers of Trebizond. Whenever he handled these blankets, Thomas had in mind the snows of unknown mountains in which one day the blankets might have to be used. To a far-Traveller, he knew, the way to Frankland would be easy; but there were high ranges on the way there. He seldom lost the chance to tip back his head outside his door and gaze at the blue-gold towers of the citadel.

'Not off yet?' Joseph would grunt when he caught him at it. 'And still using that old girth, I see.'

Yes, they were still using the old girth, with the diamond still stitched into it. It had become a superstition. The old girth had proved so safe a hiding-place for so long and so far that they did not like to replace it.

One night in the autumn the donkey began to behave oddly. Instead of eating his supper, he started steadily kicking the door of his stable, and when they went to see what was wrong did not even take the chance of stealing their supper.

'It must be the weather upsetting him,' said Thomas, peering at the strip of sky overhead. 'Blowing up for a nasty storm from the North, with a bit of West in it. Let's make up the fire.'

The donkey bunted him hard in the shoulder from behind, and at the same moment Joseph pelted down the street banging on doors and shouting, 'All out! Trouble in the harbour!'

'All right, Ears, we're *coming*!' said Thomas; but the donkey had battered the door into springing its catch and cantered out without a look behind. He turned downhill, which proved that as usual he knew what he was doing; the shortest way to the harbour was up and over the hill, but the quickest way was the longest, around the flats, so long as you knew them well enough to pick your way through the canals and water-courses. 'Oh do stop and *help*!' Thomas bellowed into the gale, and at the next little bridge, now half-brimmed-over with flood water, found the donkey waiting, though not patiently. They trotted with a hand on his quarters, and Brother James grunted between breaths, 'What trouble?'

'Small craft breaking their moorings, probably. Joseph's cousins. We should have brought a torch.'

'No, they have them on the wharves.'

They could see the torn streaming flames of a line of torches in the wharf cressets. It was not the small craft that were the trouble, though they were tossing wildly. The storm had been foreseen, and the extra moorings had held. The trouble was a big craft somewhere out in the gale that had been attempting to make harbour and failed.

'She's struck,' someone yelled in Thomas's ear as they joined the crowd under the torches. 'Get over there and join the line. We're pulling them out on the East side.'

They had made a human chain, snatching the half-drowned seamen from the sea as they were swept helplessly in. Each man in the chain braced his feet in the tugging tossing water, leant forward as a choking form was heaved into his arms by the man in front, steadied it through the next wave, and waited for the swell to heave it on to the man behind. There was shouting from the head of the line; fewer rescued men appeared, and those struggling less and choking more, and the line swayed dangerously back and forth in the swirling waves. 'She's going down!' someone shouted from seaward; and then, very deliberately, the donkey waded past the line of coughing swearing men and headed out to sea.

'Ears!' cried Thomas, and plunged after him.

'There's no one left out there!' shouted the man behind him.

The light of the torches was only some sparks behind them or a flash reflected on the upward curling of a wave. The rising waves battered Thomas around the knees, around the thighs, around the middle; he lost his footing, found it, lost it again, and floundering grasped a handful of what turned out to be the donkey. The donkey, staring out to sea, took no notice of him. 'What are you—?' coughed Thomas, and found Brother James bracing himself at his side. A flash of lightning split the sky and showed them something washing limp in the heaving sea ahead of them.

Thomas leant in to the tide, went under, came up, and cowering from the thunder that cracked tremendously overhead got one hand on the donkey's neck, swept the other into the waves, and brought up the half-drowned head of Aubery.

XXX

It was odd to have the indestructible Aubery as the invalid. He had battered ribs and a broken arm, as well as a great deal of seawater inside him, and they took him to the Street of the Golden Cockerel and put him to bed in front of the fire. The Emperor sent down a stately message of thanks to his trusty and well-beloved friends for the rescue of the honoured ambassador of his royal cousin of Georgia. It was surprising to find Aubery an honoured ambassador; but then, as Brother James pointed out, they had never expected to find themselves the trusty and well-beloved friends of an emperor. Aubery at first seemed quite sure that they were delusions, which rather took the edge off his surprise when it dawned on him that they were not. When he got restless indoors, he rode the donkey down to the allotment, and after a time found that there was work there that could be done even one-handed. As for being an ambassador of Georgia, well, yes, he supposed that was what he had been.

'Not *the* ambassador, of course. I was what they called an adviser, because I was supposed to know about the language and customs of the Franks. I found I'd forgotten most of it.' The embassy itself had been fruitless, but then the Georgians had never thought it would be anything else.

'Playing politics with the Mongols,' Thomas guessed.

'Mongol or Muslim, there isn't much to choose between them from Georgia's position. But if you've got unnerving neighbours all you can do is play them against one another.'

'I thought the Mongols were to be the saviours of Christendom,' Thomas observed.

'So did the Georgians once; so did I, you remember,' said Aubery, and gave them his shameless indestructible grin. 'We all changed our minds when the Muslims started converting the Mongols to Islam. It didn't stop the Mongols conquering them. Now if the Christians had got in first—'

Brother James said repressively, 'The Mongols would have conquered them.'

Thomas said nothing to this; but he thought that if the Christians had converted the Mongols it would inevitably have been to some kind of heresy, which would not have improved anything. 'What's really important,' he said, 'is how are they all in Georgia? Is Russudan married?'

'She turned out a handful. They wanted her to marry one of the Palaeologi of the Empire, and she took one look at him and refused. In the end she climbed out of a window one night and ran away with an ordinary colonel in the Guards. He distinguished himself in the next frontier skirmish, luckily, so they were able to forgive her. George is somewhere in the South-East, negotiating with the Sultan, a very ticklish job . . . I suppose the rest of my Georgian party went home some time ago?'

'While you were ill. You didn't want to go with them?' For the four of them had settled down nicely–if with something of a crush–in their hut, and it had never occurred to Thomas that Aubery might have other plans.

'Not really,' Aubery said vaguely. 'What happened about the Crusade, by the way?'

They told him their difficulties about the diamond.

'It's a pity I didn't know about it. But I only went as far as Rome, and no one there was interested in the East. But there's plenty of trading; you'll hear of a Cahagnes heir some time. But when I can use both hands there won't be work for all of us on one plot. Couldn't we rent another?'

That did not seem impossible, since they had a modest profit put away; but there was the partnership with Joseph to be considered. When Thomas hesitantly approached him, it turned out that he had been hesitating to approach Thomas.

'My daughter-in-law, Thomas, the one who's just had the second fine boy: you remember her father died a few months ago. They're taking over his shop by the harbour, and they want me to move in with them and help with the buying. Perhaps we could come to an arrangement about my allotment? And now there's three of you, would you want my hut?'

The arrangements about the allotment were concluded very satisfactorily; Joseph was glad of some capital to take into the shop, and Thomas and his friends were assured of an outlet for their produce. Thomas and Brother James were more doubtful about the hut, but Aubery overrode them. The extra space, he said, would be useful for storage, and he moved himself into the downstairs room at night.

Thomas had been growing more uneasy since Aubery's arrival. 'We shouldn't be so happily settled,' he said to Brother James. 'We still have the diamond. What will it be like to leave all this when we hear of the Cahagnes heir?'

'Perhaps,' said Brother James, 'the Cahagnes heir will arrive one day in Trebizond.'

Thomas had already thought of this. It seemed to him the only possible way to find a happy ending to the Donkey's Crusade; and he could not rate their chances of that very highly.

179

Since it was Brother James who dealt with their marketing, it was he who brought them the up-to-date news. Coming back with empty panniers one evening in late spring, he announced, 'A big caravan due in from Georgia soon: Joseph wants extra deliveries.'

'I'll do that,' Aubery said at once. They supposed he wanted to hear about friends left behind in Georgia, so for the next few days Brother James did the hoeing and let Aubery and the donkey load up the produce and take it into the city. One morning a week later they saw from the allotment the dust of a great caravan approaching across the plain. Aubery had the donkey loaded in record time, and took him off at a run.

Watching, hoe in hand, Brother James said meditatively, 'That appears to me curious. One expects a young man to be impatient; but what has Aubery said to Brother Donkey to make him *canter?*'

They finished the day, shouldered their tools and trudged back across the level fields, through the city gates and up the narrow alleys and stairways, with the towers of the citadel all dark-gold above them in the sunset.

'I can't get out of my mind today,' said Thomas suddenly, 'how I first saw Trebizond. In all our years of travelling, I always remembered Trebizond as the place where I would like to end my days. Which is why, these days, I am never easy in my mind.'

'Nor am I,' said Brother James surprisingly. 'That accursed diamond! On; Aubery will be waiting.'

But Aubery was not waiting. The two little huts in the Street of the Golden Cockerel were cold and empty. Thomas tutted, and kindled the fire and started supper cooking, and Brother James padded with the buckets to the well at the top of the street, which was the only one of whose water the donkey thoroughly approved; and still Aubery did not come.

'Well,' Thomas said uncertainly after a time, as the shadows fell on the narrow street, and even the strip of sky above it darkened and began to prick with stars: 'I expect he's found friends. We'll keep supper for him and the donkey.'

They sat down to eat, but being two instead of four made it curiously dismal.

'We were without Aubery for a long time,' Brother James pointed out.

'But not without the donkey,' said Thomas. He was worrying seriously now, for if the donkey deserted them it could only be for a very good reason.

It grew quite dark, and they lit the lamps, one in each hut, and Thomas went outside and put a torch in the holder between the huts.

'Why that?' asked Brother James.

'I don't know. Why are you looking over your blankets?'

Brother James had found the old blanket that had always been on the outside of his bedroll. 'There has been news, Brother Thomas; I feel it in my bones. And what news can come to us now but that the diamond must go home? I am growing old; but we must be ready.'

Thomas looked around the hut, which was warm with the fire and good-smelling with the supper, and his eyes filled with tears.

'So we must,' he said.

And suddenly there was a great noise outside, at the upper end of the Street of the Golden Cockerel, voices and laughter and steps and singing, and the solitary torch he had put up began to pale in the light of many torches coming down to it. There was the Imperial livery; and behind the Imperial livery the Most Noble David; and behind David of course the donkey, sedately picking his way down the stepped alley; and behind the donkey—

'But why is the donkey still loaded?' said Thomas.

'And who is that walking with Aubery?' said Brother James.

She was dark-haired and pale-skinned, like all the Georgians, and she was wearing her best clothes, which in the Georgian fashion were in wonderful shades of violet and rose, and the bundles in the donkey's panniers were big enough to make it clear that she had come with every intention of staying.

They came to a stop outside the huts, and Aubery, who was rocking on his feet with joy, said, 'This is Eterri. Eterri, Brother Donkey you already know; here are Brother Thomas and Brother James.'

Eterri kissed them both joyfully, and the Noble David stepped in and got the third kiss, which had probably been meant for the donkey, and the donkey signalled the joyfulness of the day by not kicking him out of the way.

'Most trusty and well-beloved friends,' said the Noble David,

181

'in this long-awaited addition to your company, I see the one thing needed to ensure your long and happy life in Trebizond. The wedding is set for tomorrow. What does the bride need to adorn herself? I claim the privilege of providing it from the Imperial Household.'

The neighbours began tumbling the bundles out of the panniers, shouting that they insisted on providing the wine, that the wife was a better hand at sweetmeats than anyone in the Palace, that they had just the real wax candles put away against such an occasion as this. Joseph suddenly appeared, panting, with his arms full of lace which he said his daughter-in-law insisted that Eterri wore at the wedding.

'In that case,' said the Noble David, beaming, heard by no one but Thomas at his side, 'nothing remains for the Imperial Household to provide but the coronet that every bride must have on her wedding day. Thomas, what shall we include in it?'

Thomas said, 'I leave it to you, Most Noble David; this is something beyond my experience. But I have two pieces of silver which I would like to see in it.'

He took him into the hut and showed him the two coins of Alexander. David looked at them with respect. 'This is your contribution to the bride's dowry? Thomas, I think it worthy of your long friendship with Aubery.' Then he became very happy, leading the way out again into the street. Like everyone in Trebizond, he loved such occasions. 'Now these will go on either side—flowers above, yes?—and Joseph's lace behind as the veil. We must find something really splendid for the centre.'

And there in the street stood the donkey, and the worn old girth that held the panniers at his side split at last. The leather crumbled, the panniers spilt right and left, and at the side of the donkey fell the buckle and its stitching. A scrap of scarlet silk uncurled and became dust, and among the cobbles lay and flashed the diamond of the Sieur de Cahagnes.

'The diamond!' gasped Thomas, reeling on to Brother James's arm.

The Noble David picked it up. 'Well, not really,' he said. 'A nicely cut stone, I grant you, and will look exactly right in the centre of the bridal coronet; but nothing but rock-crystal. It should be set in silver, don't you agree? I shall take it back to the

Palace and return tomorrow with it properly set.'

And then it became a party which involved the whole of the Street of the Golden Cockerel, so that there was not much more to be said.

What there was to be said Thomas and Brother James managed to say about two in the morning, when David disentangled them from the dancing and singing to say that he really must go or the bridal coronet would never be ready for the wedding.

'It's not that we doubt you,' said Thomas, steadying himself with an effort—he had not drunk too much of the wine the neighbours had brought out, but he was finding that joy and unsettlement and relief were worse than wine for making steps unsteady and words confused. 'But we both knew the Sieur de Cahagnes, rest his soul, and we know he believed that his stone was a gift worthy to be given by Christendom to Prester John.'

'Who did not exist.' The Noble David hiccuped a little and straightened his Imperial insignia. 'Dear me, your neighbours do know how to set up a party at short notice, don't they? I haven't enjoyed myself so much for years. Oh my dear Thomas—my dear Brother James—of course your Sieur de Cahagnes was entirely honest: if just a little naïve. This so-called diamond was a treasure in his family, yes? Given by the Emperor of Byzantium at the time of the First Crusade, yes? Well, you know, there are very few families who don't at some time or other run into financial difficulties. And then they pawn the diamond; and what could be more sensible then than to have it copied in some cheaper stone, to preserve their credit; and then they never recover quite completely enough to redeem the diamond, but does it really matter, seeing that they have the copy and the credit? Believe me, there are not many heirlooms of great families which can stand up against the trained eye. Even the Imperial family—but I believe I was on the verge of committing treason. Is it really important? It's very pretty and will make your brother's quite enchanting bride look even lovelier. I find myself uncertain whether we should not plan the coronet so that she can wear her hair high in the Trebizond fashion. What do you think? She is going to live her life in Trebizond now, after all.'

Brother James retreated, waving his hand to indicate that he

183

had no views to offer on such frivolous matters. Thomas looked down the Street of the Golden Cockerel to where Eterri sat on her bundles, with Aubery glowing beside her and her eyes bright and her smile kind, and said with all his heart, 'She should always look just as she looks now.'

'What a sensible view!' said the Most Noble David, and took the stone and the two silver coins and the lace, not too steadily, away up the steep streets of Trebizond to the towers of the citadel.

The party in the Street of the Golden Cockerel showed no sign of stopping, except that the donkey trotted up to join them. Brother James said, 'Aubery and Eterri will have Joseph's hut, of course, and as soon as the children come along we can build an upper floor to it. They will be short of cooking-pots. If we promised Leah free vegetables for a week, she might find them pots enough tomorrow.'

And he went down to find Leah.

Thomas and the donkey stayed where they were. They could see the party, but the blue dawn was coming up, and they could see also the towers of Trebizond beginning to shine blue-gold against the sky, and beyond them the fading pearl-blue levels of the lands of Trebizond.

'Yes, well, Ears,' said Thomas. He was not used to having nothing to worry about. 'Aubery seems very happy, and that's a charming girl he's going to marry, and we're nicely settled and the neighbours are contented. But is it a proper ending for all that we've been through, with its kings and its kingdoms?'

The donkey looked down at the party, and swung his heavy head to Thomas and spoke. As it turned out, it was the last time in Thomas's life that he found it necessary to do this (though donkeys live for a long time, and there is no saying whether or not he decided to guide the ways of the children of Aubery and Eterri). All he had to say was: 'Remember!' And Thomas remembered: the courteous golden man Li Pao; and the fish-villagers and the good idolatrous people; and the music-lover Hliakh; and the incorporeal spirit in the desert; and the old war-horse left at Belle-Désirée; and his three ladies in the swamp-fields; and the crippled old Traveller in Tiflis, and the red-bearded Traveller with the peppery dark wine, and two caravan masters, and George and Russudan, and many many others. But mostly he remembered his donkey, in the camp beyond the desert of the incorporeal spirits, looking mildly at him to remind him what it was to be a donkey, to carry out his business in life, and to take pride in doing it well.

'We've fulfilled our contract, Brother Donkey,' he said. 'And you've a wedding to attend in the morning and your girth's broken. Come down to the hut and I'll make you a new one.'